P|

Fall Into You

If When Harry Met Sally is the quintessential fall movie, Fall Into You is the quintessential fall book. So many quirky, funny episodes, romantic scenes and steamy, heart-racing moments.

— Amazon Reviewer

I loved, loved, loved this book! It has spice, it has the brother's best friend trope, and it has the instalove, but done in a way that doesn't make me cringe. Liza and Matt's chemistry is over the top awesome, and I'm insanely excited to see that it is book one in a series!

— @RomanceBooksFan

If you're looking for a rom-com with a Fall feeling, look no further  I'm looking forward to the next install-ment in the series.

— @Lissthebooklover

PRAISE FOR
Shall We Dance?

This book easily moved to my favorite rom com spot. Barbara and Theo are such a fun couple. I'm a sucker for enemies to lovers and Caroline Frank did a wonderful job nailing this with the perfect amount of banter, spice, and tension. I found myself thinking about this story constantly, and couldn't wait to finish it, but also wanted to savor every word.

— @vicwiththegoodbooks

This book is everything a romance novel should be. It had all the pieces for a perfect love story. Enemies to lovers, grump and sunshine, and a detrimental miss communication. What more could a romance lover want?? I loved the characters and how real and relatable they were. Shall We Dance is a 10/10.

— Amazon reviewer

I'm swooning over this book!

— JenG

Happily Ever Disaster

SEASONS OF LOVE:
BOOK 2.5

CAROLINE FRANK

For all the Matt and Liza fans out there.
And the Fall lovers, of course.

Author's Note

The idea of Liza and Matt's wedding initially started off as a bonus epilogue chapter, no more than 3,000 words, intended for those who signed up to my newsletter.

But then... Then I remembered how lovely Matt is and how much he and Liza love each other. I remembered Danielle and Vinny (and my God, I'm dying to write a prequel about them one day), and Barbara and Theo and I thought... No. I *have* to write something a *little* longer.

So it grew into two chapters. But then... I wanted to add spice. So I did that.

And then... I was so anxious to introduce Rosie's story (because it's so incredibly sweet and romantic) and I thought ***spoiler alert*** "Wouldn't it be fun to introduce her POV at the end of the book?". And oh, it was.

In the end, it grew into what it is now—too long to be called a "bonus chapter" and certainly too short to be called a book. So I wondered, what do I do with this?

Publish it as a teeny novella.

Also, please enjoy the first few chapters of Seasons of Love Book 3: Second Chance Snowman!

Anyway, I hope you enjoy this brief little chapter of where our loved characters are now.

Much love,

CF

To keep up with the latest author news, make sure you sign up to my newsletter by clicking here. You'll have the most up-to-date info on giveaways, new releases, blog posts, and bonus content!

Chapter One

LIZA

"We should really stop." But I say the words against Matt's lips, and scoot even closer, my hand fisting tighter in his hair, pulling his mouth down to my neck.

"Yes. We should." But he groans, his right hand reaching to swing both of my legs over his thighs in one rough, quick movement. His fingers dig into my dress, tugging me into him, his hard cock just beneath me.

It's not the most comfortable of positions, but there aren't very many options in the backseat of a small compact car when you have a car-seat next to you. It's also *especially* difficult when you're trying hard *not* to let things escalate.

"We should stop," I say again. But he presses his lips to mine, his tongue swirling suggestively in my mouth in a way that makes me so dizzy, it almost knocks me unconscious. I know *exactly* what other things he does with that tongue.

Wow, okay. We really *need to stop.*

But we can't help ourselves.

The scent of his cologne, concentrated in the small,

enclosed space, the memory of how freaking incredible he looked tonight during the rehearsal dinner in that crisp suit, and the feel of his mouth and hands on me, has my head spinning. The usual fog that comes whenever Matt touches me like that has clouded my judgment, but I can't bring myself to care too much.

"It feels so good, though," I say. My voice sounds so breathy and desperate, for a second, I think the words come from someone else.

Matt groans, his hand traveling to the inside of my thighs now, sliding slowly, torturously. "You wanted this," he murmurs into my ear. His fingers are just a few inches from where I want him to be—*need* him to be.

I can barely inhale before replying, "*Me?*"

He nods against me, his lips grazing the delicate skin of my neck. "You were the one who thought *celibacy* a month before the wedding would be a great idea." The dreaded C word comes out with mock-disgust, and I let out a breathless laugh at his frustration.

"Well," a sharp inhale when he grazes a thumb over my underwear in just the right spot. "You were dumb enough to agree. You're supposed to be the smart one in the relationship."

He snorts and tugs my earlobe lightly with his teeth. "*Me,* the smart one? C'mon. We both know that isn't true. Especially not when it comes to you. You know I would do anything you asked me to." His voice seems to lose some of its levity in that last sentence. He stops kissing me suddenly, and rests his head on my shoulder for a minute. I lean back to look at him, placing my hand on his cheek, tilting his face back up towards mine, forcing him to meet my eyes.

"What is it?"

"I would, you know. Do anything for you." Something tugs at my heart in that painful, yet pleasurable way that comes with loving someone so much your lungs feel like they have something wrapped tightly around them, making it impossible to breathe. "It's why I agreed to this stupid fucking plan," he almost growls.

I smile at him and kiss him softly on the lips for only a second. He furrows his brows, leaning towards me for more, but I place my palm on his chest and stop him. "I will admit that in retrospect, this whole celibacy pact thing hasn't been as romantic as I thought it would be. It mostly just feels like the world's longest, drawn out foreplay ever, at this point." He chuckles at my own frustration, evident in the whining tone of my voice. "I would've been okay getting married at City Hall, for the record. I would've been happy going out to get a great burger after, just the two of us and Lucy. You're the one who wanted this stupid wedding in the first place—who pushed me into it. I am of the opinion that we didn't need one."

He grabs the hand still resting on his chest and brings its palm to his lips, kissing it gently. "I pushed you—if that's even the right word—into this wedding because I knew you'd regret it later in life if we didn't have any type of celebration. And I knew it would be even more special to have it in the fall at *Tom's*. After all, it's where our story began." He flashes that heartbreaking smile of his at me and brings my hand to his lips again, kissing each of my knuckles before reaching up to cup my jaw. "Maybe we didn't *need* one, but I *wanted* one—for both of us."

My heart squeezes in my chest at his heartbreaking smile. He ducks his head to kiss up my neck again, and I feel myself melt in his arms once more, pliant. "I guess you're right."

"Hmm."

"Though I think it might've been nice to wait another year instead of spontaneously deciding to do this thing just a few months ago."

"No. I was done waiting. Needed to lock this thing down once and for all." I want to laugh at how ridiculous he sounds, tell him we have a kid together for God's sake, but a shiver runs down my spine at the possessive tone in his voice, at the bite he places on my neck. And anyway, I can see his point, since the thought of officially being able to call him *mine* brings me a cavewoman-like joy I've only ever experienced since dating him.

My husband. *My* daughter. *My* family.

I smile into the low-lit car while Matt continues to attack my neck with his mouth—kissing it, sucking at it, teeth grazing my skin. I want to stay in the moment, but thinking of our little family takes me from filling me with an overwhelming feeling of happiness to one of anxiety.

"I hope Lucy is okay," I whisper, biting my lower lip.

"Catterina's babysat before," he mumbles into my skin before inhaling as if my perfume were the most delicious scent in the world. "She'll be great."

But I bite my lip, unconvinced. Mom is amazing with Lucy, but my baby is spending the next couple of nights at my mom's, and the idea has had me on edge for the past few days. One night alone with my mom doesn't make me anxious, but it will be several days of being without her. Lucy is there tonight to make sure I'm well-rested before the wedding. Then, she'll be spending a few more days with my mom while Matt and I go away for our mini-moon. We won't be far, having chosen to go out to an inn in Montauk about two hours away. But the idea of leaving my baby girl for the first time without either of us grips my heart and makes me feel selfish.

Matt feels my body tense, and pulls back, his hand coming up to cup my jaw. "Hey. Seriously. She's not a newborn anymore—Lucy will be perfect. No mom guilt tonight, please. We *need* this alone time together, babe." His brows furrow, green eyes pleading with me. "I feel like we never get any of it

4

anymore. And I don't want to sound like a needy asshole here, but we haven't had sex in a month, Liza. *A month.* And I'm pretty sure I'm dying from it." He groans, a desperate sound, and I laugh, because we've definitely gone through longer dry spells than this—especially during the last stretch of my pregnancy and the first couple of months after Lucy was born.

But still. It's not my pregnancy or postpartum recovery keeping us away from each other this time around. Just a silly pact that popped into my head one day, which I thought would be incredibly romantic.

I run my fingers through his disheveled hair, pushing it neatly back into place. "I know," I giggle, feeling a mild sense of accomplishment at the desperation in his voice.

"I spent all night at dinner just looking at you, thinking about tomorrow. You're so beautiful." He swallows hard once, his gaze so intense, I feel a flush cover every inch of my body. "I can't believe this is finally happening."

Emotion clogs my throat, eyes stinging. I move closer to him, looping my arms around his neck, and press my forehead to his, our lips just inches apart. "I love you," I tell him, my voice soft.

His smile is almost blinding, even in the dark of the night. He closes the distance between our lips and gives me a deep kiss, reigniting the consuming need for him—for *this*.

The look of tenderness in Matt's eyes turns into one of hunger and then: "I can't wait to fuck you." His voice is gravelly, rough. I almost laugh at his sudden change in tone, but his hands grip my hips and he readjusts me, positioning my legs on either side of his, my skirt riding up my legs as I straddle him.

"You're so romantic," I tease, kissing up his neck to his jaw. Feeling his hardness between my thighs, I roll my hips tentatively, essentially dry-humping him in the backseat of the rental. Matt squeezes his eyes shut and throws his head back with a groan, hands tightening on my hips, while I revel in the feeling of his fingers pressing into my skin. My intention was to torture him, but the heat building low between my legs has increased, and feeling him hard, rubbing me just right, is clouding my judgement. My basic instincts crying out for him.

Need him. Need him now.

Matt's hand glides slowly up my thigh again, raising goose-bumps all over my body. So slow, I consider whether he's doing it on purpose to torture me. They travel under the skirt of my dress and he lifts it, pushing me back just a little to look down. "*Fuck,*" he almost growls, running a finger under the elastic of my black lace thong. "It's a good thing we're getting married tomorrow, because I don't think I can take much longer before I spontaneously combust. You've been teasing me around the house this past week, wearing all this crazy lingerie." He snaps the elastic once before running his fingers underneath it again.

I lean over and unbutton the top three buttons of his shirt as I kiss him under his jaw. I hear his ragged breathing in my ear, growing faster when I dip my hand under the fabric of his shirt, feeling his warm chest underneath my fingertips, hard and soft all at the same time.

"You think those sets were crazy? Wait till you see the ones I brought for our mini-moon." I smirk, wanting his imagination to run wild.

He groans, fisting his hands tightly in my underwear, and I hear a small tear. "*Fuck. Fuck, fuck.*" A big smile spreads across my face, feeling almost victorious.

Honestly? I love that I can still drive him crazy like this.

He pulls his hand away from me and checks his watch before saying, "You know—" But his mind wanders as my tongue travels up his neck.

"Hmm?" I press my lips to him once more and moving my hips over his hardness again, never stopping, feeling myself lose any sense of control I had left with each passing second.

"*Fuck*, Liza—*Agh.*" But he grabs hold of my hips with both hands and pulls me hard and fast into him, a shot of pleasure running through me. "It's—It's almost midnight. Practically our wedding day. We could—"

But I don't let him even finish the sentence before my hands drop into his lap to unbuckle his pants and unzip his fly. Matt doesn't waste any time either, immediately reaching around my back to unzip my dress, moving my hands away from him long enough to pull my arms from its sleeves. I grind on him and we groan, both already so, so close.

Suddenly, the awareness that we're about to have sex in a dark parking lot like a couple of teenagers pops into my head, but I could not care less.

Matt pulls down the cups of my bra, and sucks a nipple into his mouth, while pinching and twisting the other with his fingers. He uses his free hand to help rock me against him, while I start to lose my mind.

"Oh my God," I dig my hand into his hair before pushing his head away. "Need you now."

"Yes," he groans. I reach down to his pants and push them as low as I can before digging my hand into his boxers and—

A bright light flashes into the car, cutting the moment short just before there's a knock on the passenger window.

A MAN WHO LOOKS TO BE IN HIS FIFTIES IN A GREY ZIP-UP jacket with the yellow words *Security* emblazoned in the front bends and peers into the window, glaring at us.

"Shit! Cover yourself up!" Matt moves as fast as he can to form a sort of protective cover around me with his arms. Immediately, I adjust my bra and pull my dress up to cover myself, wanting to die. After I've managed to put myself together (if that's what you call it), Matt pulls my skirt down, using it to cover *himself* up. I almost tell him it's no use, that *of course* the freedom guard knows exactly what we were doing—what we were *about* to do. There's no hiding it and there's no way the guy didn't get a look at the goods, but I guess trying to maintain *some* sort of decency helps.

At least for his peace of mind, anyway.

Matt leans over to open the passenger window. "Hey, there," he clears his throat, trying to remain calm and collected. Meanwhile, I struggle to stifle hysterical laughter while I consider entering the witness protection program.

In a thick Long Island accent, I hear the guard address Matt. "Sir, this ain't that type of '*parking*' zone," he chides.

"Oh, God," I groan, hiding my face in my hands.

"I don't wanna have to call the police on ya."

"No!" Matt raises his hands in the air. "Please, no. We're— We're guests of the inn. We're getting married tomorrow, and most of our guests from out of town are staying here. I'm sorry, sir. We'll—*Agh.*" I squirm in Matt's lap, wanting more than anything to get the hell out of here. "*Stop that,*" he whispers low in my ear, understanding dawning on me. I flush an even deeper shade of crimson.

The guard rolls his eyes at Matt. "Just get yourselves dressed and outta my parking lot, will ya? I'm gonna take a walk around the lot, and when I come back, I don't wanna see you here, got it?"

"Yes, sir." Matt nods vehemently, and the security walks away. He mutters something under his breath that sounds like "Who do they think they are, a bunch of teenagers or something?".

We finish dressing in record time, our breathing still labored from being in the heat of the moment. Together, we stumble out of the car and back into the inn on shaky legs.

Holding hands, Matt and I climb the stairs together all the way to the second floor landing, where we stop to say goodnight.

He wraps his arms around me and presses a soft kiss on my forehead. "I love you," he whispers, keeping a low voice so as not to wake other guests.

A slow smile spreads across my face. "I love you, too."

Matt kisses me with another drugging kiss, which quickly turns into desperate and hungry. He walks me backwards and presses me up against the closest wall. His hand trails down my side and over my thigh, where he stops to pull my leg up below my knee, hooking it over his hip. Matt presses his hardness into me, and I moan into his mouth.

He pulls his face back just an inch, but his lips graze over mine as he says in an almost agonized voice, "I love you so much, Liza." I inhale sharply, my rib cage expanding with emotion. He's said it a dozen times today, but this time it feels weighted somehow. "I feel like my chest is about to explode from it. Do you ever feel that way?" He frowns, curious.

"Only all the time," I whisper.

He chuckles softly before pushing into me once more. "I will always love you, and I want you to know that you've made me the happiest guy on the planet. *But*"—I feel my body tense at his infinitesimal pause—"I also want you to know that, despite feeling all gooey and mushy right now, I fully intend to fuck the shit out of you as soon as possible. I'll make love to you after the fact."

I laugh-snort and shake my head at his desperation, trying to keep it down. Matt leans his head into where my neck meets my shoulder and chuckles against me. He inhales deeply and holds his breath for a few seconds before whispering, "I'll miss you tonight."

I pull away and hold his head in my hands, tugging him in for a chaste kiss. "Me, too. Love you."

With a resigned sigh, he reluctantly drops my leg and puts some space between us. I feel the loss of the warmth of his body against every inch of mine with a pang in my stomach, a wave of sadness at our brief separation falling over me.

Feeling completely ridiculous, I squeeze his hand before walking away on trembling legs, stopping only to look over my shoulder once just as I step into my bedroom alone.

Chapter Two

LIZA

"Ow! You just stabbed me!" I squirm away from Rosie as she attempts to sew on one of three buttons that popped off about twenty minutes ago. I had already put on my dress and knew I had to be careful, but Lucy was begging I play with her, so I caved and ended up ruining it less than an hour before the ceremony.

Thank God for Rosie, who swept in and saved the day. She's an amazing costume designer on *Celebrity Dance Battle*, that TV show where Barbara met her fiancé Theo, so she was able to help.

"I wouldn't accidentally be stabbing you if you'd keep still," she mutters, her words barely understandable as she holds a needle between her teeth. She crouches behind me again in the middle of our makeshift bridal suite—the farm owner's main office.

"Hey, you try carrying the world's cutest kid in your arms while someone's sewing a button on you." I look down at Lucy and bounce her on my hip, trying to be gentle enough not to tear at the delicate beading that covers my entire dress.

11

Lucy is a little antsy right now, but that's to be expected considering all the commotion around us. I watch her as she lays her head on my chest, holding a strand of my hair in one hand, tugging at it—and my heart—lightly.

Rosie smiles ruefully up at me as she kneels by my feet, her pastel pink hair done up in a perfect, braided bun at the base of her neck. I admire the intricacies of it as she adjusts another button and take in her outfit—a bohemian chic mauve dress made from the most delicate lace I've ever seen in my life.

Since meeting her through Barbara, and quickly becoming close friends soon thereafter, I've come to realize a few things about Rosie: first, she always, *always* wears pink—in some shape, way, or form.

Second, like my family, hers also revolves a lot around food. *A lot.* Turns out Latin American families and Italian families are more similar than you'd think.

And third, when it comes to her, if it can be bedazzled, it will be bedazzled—as is evidenced by the pink heart-shaped sunglasses she was wearing earlier today. And her shoes. And her sparkly clutch. Honestly, it was so much sparkle I damn near needed my own sunglasses just to look at her.

But she pulls it off, easy-peasy.

"Fair enough, but maybe you should put her down? Hand her over to your mom?" I glare at her, pulling my baby closer to me. Lucy pulls at my hair, and I gently release the strand from her superhuman strength baby fists.

"*No.* I'm not putting her down. I'm really nervous and holding her keeps me calm." Except when she's having one of her tantrums, of course (how am I supposed to keep up with the ever-changing tastes of my almost-toddler's palate?)

I hear a snort from behind, and my eyes fly open to find Danielle smirking at me. "It's a little too late to be nervous about marrying Matt, don't you think?" She shakes her head and laughs. "I mean, not to point out the obvious, but you do realize that you and your husband-to-be have been living together for almost two years now? *And that you have a child together?*"

My sister-in-law has always been incredible at stating the obvious. I want to say something snarky, but I can't give her too much crap considering how much she helped me and Matt out during the early days of our relationship while we were still secretly dating. It wasn't easy hiding it from Vinny, my older brother and Matt's best friend, but she helped us date in secret while we figured out how we felt about each other exactly. That is until Vinny found out and everything kind of blew up in our faces.

Danielle got into a lot of trouble for lying to my brother just to help me, so I do owe her a lot. I might not even be here if it weren't for her. Still, I roll my eyes at her and look down at Lucy —perfect, beautiful Lucy—who grabs at another strand of my hair, pulling much harder this time.

"Ow!"

"Uh-oh." My mother runs quickly over to me, her arms splayed in front of her. "Okay. Rosie's right. Give me the baby. She's going to ruin your dress and hair. Plus, it's my responsibility to take care of her today, anyway."

Lucy stretches her arms out towards her *Nonna* with an eager smile. I whimper as my mother takes my daughter from me, wanting to follow them to the big arm chair in the corner of the room where she sits her on her lap. But no. I'm stuck here until Rosie's done sewing me up.

I just want to hold her again.

It's weird this whole motherhood thing. Unconditional love.

But then again, I feel it with Matt. A different type of love, obviously. But the same in the sense that it feels completely endless; that there's nothing that would ever make it stop.

My heart squeezes in my chest as I think of how I finally get to marry him today, how we're less than an hour away from making it official.

Matt proposed over a year ago over Christmas, just a couple of days after finding out I was pregnant with Lucy, but we wanted to wait to have our little girl be present since she was already on her way. After a while, though, we kind of put getting married on the back burner. It wasn't until around July when Matt got impatient, that he suggested we do it this fall. So we did. We planned a small wedding at Tom's Pumpkin Farm, the same place where we fell in love at second sight almost two years ago to the day.

Two years.

It doesn't feel like it, to be honest. So much has happened since we were here last. The secret dating, Vinny losing his mind when he found out about us, Matt getting his butt kicked by him. Then, finding out I was pregnant—which was an amazing surprise. Us getting engaged and me moving into his place. Graduating from grad school and having Lucy. My new job at a non-profit offering free-counseling services to at-risk teens.

It's been a wild ride, that's for sure.

"I'm not nervous about marrying Matt." I roll my eyes again, scoffing at the ridiculous suggestion that I would ever, for even just one second, have any doubts about being with him. The man is basically perfection. Six-foot three, perfect haired, green eyed, best dad, sweet as candy, amazing-in-bed perfection. "I'm nervous of all the people out there, watching me walk down that aisle. What if I trip on my dress and fall flat on my face?"

"You're not going to fall flat on your face," a voice interrupts me. I turn to it, and my smile broadens automatically at the sight of my best friend.

"Oh my god! You made it! I thought you were only going to be able to make the reception!"

Holding a bottle of champagne in one hand, Barbara grins broadly as she looks me up and down with something akin to pride in her eyes. "I snuck out of dress rehearsal super early, but I'm sure they won't notice."

"Aren't you the lead in the play? Won't you get in trouble?" Danielle asks, but we ignore her. Who cares whether she gets in trouble or not? She's here! She's here!

I try to go to her, but Rosie pulls my hand to keep me still. Noticing this, Barbara runs toward me and pulls me into a delicate hug. "I really want to give you a big bear hug or whatever, but I don't want to ruin anything. You look perfect."

"Step away from the delicately beaded dress," Rosie's soft voice is laced with venom as she narrows her eyes at Barbara. To my surprise, my best friend immediately obeys, slowly and carefully pulling away. Danielle and I snort in amusement.

"You look perfect." I notice Barbara's eyes water and I stare at her in shock.

"Are you— Are you *crying?*" I balk, somewhat horrified. No. There's no way.

"No. Shut up. *You're* crying." But she wipes the back of her hand over nose and sniffs once.

"Oh my god," Danielle groans. "You're *allowed* to get emotional at weddings. It's like a rule. Let yourselves be emotional." She shakes her head at the both of us. "Now, where are the glasses for that champagne?"

"Where's Theo?"

Barbara waves her hand dismissively. "He's already sitting in the audience, I think."

I nod just when Rosie finishes sewing the final button. "There. I'm done." She gets to her feet and puts her hands on her waist, eying me from top to bottom. "Thank god it wasn't a big fix! I mean, of things that can go wrong at a wedding, this is definitely the least concerning."

Ever the superstitious Italian, my mother's eyes widen in fear with a tiny gasp. The absolute terror that flashes before her eyes at the thought that Rosie just jinxed the wedding goes unnoticed by everyone but me. I stare intently at her and mouth, "*Relax.* Please."

She looks back at me with concern, chewing her bottom lip, but I roll my eyes in exasperation.

I will not let little things like this get to me on my wedding day. She's being ridiculous.

Trying to keep it together as I feel the nerves rise within me, I take a deep, settling breath as Barbara and Danielle work as a team to pour everyone a glass of champagne. But when I get mine, I look at the golden bubbly liquid with hesitation.

"What's wrong?" Danielle asks.

I grimace. "I don't want to drink tonight. I had some champagne last night at the rehearsal dinner after not having any alcohol in months, and—"

And ended up getting caught hardcore-making out with Matt in the backseat of my car like a horny teenager.

But of course I don't say that.

"And. Well. Got a little tipsy. I don't want to be a drunk bride. So tacky. Like I said, I'm not used to alcohol anymore—haven't had it in months before last night—and am not sure whether it's a good idea given the occasion."

"Yeah, I guess there are a lot of *things* your body might not be physically used to anymore." Barbara snickers and wiggles her eyebrows suggestively before handing a glass to Rosie. I blush bright red and my mother slaps my best friend on the arm. It doesn't take a genius to understand what she meant.

"Inappropriate, Barbara," my mother hisses.

"Yes, Catterina. You're right. I'm sorry." But when my mother turns her back on us, my idiot friends burst out into a fit of laughter.

"You seriously haven't had sex since you guys started planning the wedding?" Danielle asks quietly, making sure neither my mom nor Lucy overhears her.

I blush an even deeper shade of red, and even though I know she's whispering and my mother is out of earshot, I'm painfully aware of her presence.

"Not since we started *planning* it. It's just been a month." The longest month of my freaking life. My face heats even more as I regret ever telling them anything. I turn away to look at myself in the mirror, trying to keep my voice to a whisper. "We stupidly thought it would be romantic to wait until the wedding. Or I did, I guess. He was supportive at first, but I think he's close to losing it." I smirk, thinking of last night. My fingers touch my lips, where I can practically still feel his near-bruising kiss.

I watch Barbara roll her eyes in the mirror, a little teasing smile on her face. "You guys have a *child*. You *live* together. You are literally doing everything conventionally backwards. Why stop now? Who cares *what* you do? It's your lives."

"It's not about that," I tell her. "We want to make it romantic. So I thought, why not wait a little? Have a little build up. We want the first time we do it as a married couple to be special." Although, given what Matt said last night, I highly doubt it'll be rose petals and candlelit mood lighting.

Barbara rolls her eyes at me and turns to everyone else. "Okay, everybody gather round." Mom sets Lucy down, who runs straight over to her stroller to get one of her toys. She immediately come back to me, reaching for my hand. I take hers in mine and smile down at her as the adults all gather round with a glass of champagne. "Let's raise a glass to Matt and Liza, who have had the weirdest, winding road to get here."

"*Unconventional—not weird*," I correct her.

"Whatever. To Matt and Liza! And to them finally—" her eyes drop nervously to Lucy, who's staring up at her with adoration. "Um, to them finally kissing each other again." My daughter looks up at me in confusion, but doesn't say anything.

"Here, here!" Danielle calls, raising her glass and taking a generous sip.

Rosie giggles into her drink while my mother shakes her head disapprovingly at Barbara and Danielle. But mostly Barbara.

My best friend catches the expression on my mother's face and smiles. "Come on, *Mamma Castelli*. It's just a joke."

A total softy for my eccentric friend, my mom reluctantly smiles up at her and takes a sip of her own glass.

Just then, someone knocks on the door. *"Can I come in? It's John."*

Rosie looks at me questioningly. "The owner of the farm," I whisper.

"I thought his name was Tom. Isn't that what this place is called? Tom's?"

"No. That was his grandfather. The one who started it."

"Uh, I can... I can hear you. This is an old building, and the walls aren't exactly soundproof."

The girls burst out laughing while I roll my eyes. "Come in."

Rosie opens the door for him, but he freezes in the doorway. His wide eyes are on her, his body completely unmoving, slack-jawed.

I smile to myself, because I get it. Right now, Rosie looks almost ethereal. Like a fairy straight out of one of those fantasy romance novels that have become so popular.

"John?" I interrupt his gawking. "You were saying?"

"What?" He mumbles, his eyes never leaving my friend— who looks a little uncomfortable.

"Can I help you?" I hear Danielle and Barbara snicker in the background, laughing at the poor, enamored man.

"Uh, yeah. Sorry." He flushes, turning to look at me for the

18

first time since opening the door. "Just wanted to let you know that we're ready when you are."

I feel the butterflies in my stomach go wild, my breathing speed.

This is it.

An uncontrollable smile spreads across my face in anticipation. "Great. Can you get my brother, please? He'll be the one walking me down the aisle."

From the hallway, I can hear my brother yell out an enthusiastic "Present!" I sigh in relief, the nerves bubbling up in my system once more at the thought of having to walk down that aisle in front of my friends and family. "Vincenzo Castelli in the house! Where my little sister at?"

Chapter Three

LIZA

Vinny moves around John, squeezing by into the room.

"We should be good to go in a couple of minutes," I say, gently running my hands over the material of my dress over my hips.

John nods before checking his watch. "Okay, I'm going to do a final walk-through, then, and come back when you're ready."

"Thanks, John." He gives me a hesitant smile before walking away.

To be honest, I was scared about having my wedding here. They'd never hosted one before, and planning it—especially in just a few months—was a bit of a crazy experience. But when it came down to the venue, there was no other place we thought would be more perfect than this one.

I hear a sharp gasp behind me and jump. Startled, I turn to watch my brother run over to the coffee table in the middle of the room. "Is that champagne? *Sick!* I was just with the other groomsmen and we didn't have any alcohol in there. *Super* lame." Vinny pours himself a generous helping of champagne, killing the bottle off.

"*And* you have a cheese board?" My brother's eyes go wide at the assortment of cheese and crackers sitting next to our make-shift makeup table. Immediately, Vinny starts piling crackers and pieces of cheese on a small plate, his tongue sticking out of the corner of his mouth.

Danielle clears her throat. "Excuse me? Are you going to say hi to me at some point?" She asks pointedly.

Vinny turns quickly around and jogs happily with his full plate over to his wife. "Hey, babe." He wraps an arm around her waist, pulling her in for a kiss. "You look absolutely beautiful," he whispers in her ear. The moment escalates into one of more intimacy than we expected, and I turn away when Danielle blushes. My heart warms thinking that, even though they annoy the hell out of each other a lot of the time and even though they've been together for so long, Vinny and Danielle still sometimes act like they're going through their honeymoon period.

I hope Matt and I always stay the same, too, while growing together.

"Thanks," she mumbles. After a few seconds, she seems to recover and comes back to her normal self. "Where are the kids, by the way? I thought you were watching them."

"Nah. They're with Matt," he shrugs, taking another sip. "He's babysitting."

My sister-in-law inhales sharply. "Vinny! Matt cannot be babysitting. Matt is getting *married* in a few minutes." Danielle's voice rises, quickly turning irritated.

I look at him like he's lost his mind. Is he for real? "Matt can't be responsible for the twins when he needs to be focused on the fact that he's getting married in less than half an hour."

Mom slaps him on the arm, just like she did with Barbara. "*Vincenzo!*"

"Ow. *Jesus.* Guys, relax. They're fine. He doesn't need to *focus.*" He rolls his eyes at us. "Matt's getting married, not

21

taking a test. Plus, his mom said she'd send them over right before we were supposed to go on. The twins need to walk down the aisle, too, remember? The flower girl and ring bearer? We're good. It's just for a couple of minutes."

Danielle rolls her eyes and walks away, arms crossed in front of her chest, while I grimace. Though Matt's mom has become more involved in her son's life since my pregnancy, wanting to be part of our daughter's life too, I still don't trust her maternal instincts. I mean, what kind of woman practically abandons her son after losing his father? Matt's mom wasn't there for him emotionally, and even though she says she's changed, it still makes me scared for him *and* my daughter.

"It'll *all* be fine, you'll see." My brother pats Danielle's hand, trying to calm her down, not realizing his actions have the opposite effect.

Doing my best to push it out of my mind, I exhale slowly and look at myself in the mirror. My long brown hair has been blown out and pulled back into a gorgeous half-do made up of intricate braids my mom worked on for hours earlier today. Danielle did my makeup and managed to make me look natural, but glowy. And my dress... my dress is everything I dreamed of and then some.

Because we planned this so short-notice, I didn't really have much to work with. But as fate would have it, while walking through Brooklyn after brunch with the girls and Lucy, we ran into the most adorable bridal boutique.

Each dress in there looked like it was plucked from a scene from *A Midsummer Night's Dream* or something. Sheer fabrics combined with delicate beading and even more delicate lace filled the store, and we just knew there had to be something in here for me.

Lo-and-behold, on the mannequin in the middle of the little boutique was the same dress I wear now: a long-sleeved cream piece made of embroidered lace with a modest v neckline in the front and not-too-poofy skirt with a slight train. Beaded with small iridescent white seed beads over certain lace flowers, the dress has a flattering A-line shape that makes me look slim and somehow taller.

On top of all the incredible hand-sewn details and work put into the dress that make it unique and special, it has a super-sexy deep open back which is my present to Matt (though I have to admit I'm scared of freezing to death out there because of it.

"All right. Let's get going, then." Vinny tosses back the rest of his champagne and leads the cohort out of the room. Danielle and Barbara help me by holding the train as we make our way out. From the doorway, I turn and watch as mom takes Lucy's hand, but not before helping her put on a pretty petticoat to keep her warm.

The rest of us, I'm positive, will probably freeze a little in the cold fall air.

Still holding Lucy's hand, my mom turns to look at me with a smile and wipes at her eyes. "Your father would be so proud of you, Liza. And though I know we all wish he were physically here, I'm pretty certain that I can feel him everywhere today."

She reaches out to grab my hand and gives it a squeeze just as I feel myself choke up.

I miss him every day, but today has been especially hard. I thought the day I'd miss him the most would be Lucy's birth, but I've gotta say it pales in comparison. It's tradition for a dad to walk his daughter down the aisle, and mine won't get to do that.

The pain slices through me, knocking me almost breathless. The whole idea of doing this without him killed me, to the point that I almost didn't want to have a wedding at all. I wanted to go to City Hall, where there was no pressure to do anything like that. But in the end, I know that's not what my father would've wanted for me, which is why we decided to have a small wedding here.

"I wish he could've seen how great of a mother you are. And how you're going to make a great wife, as well."

I pull away from my friends and wrap my arms tightly around my mother. "Thanks, mom."

I squeeze my eyes shut, doing my best to hold in the tears, when Vinny's voice interrupts us. "Uh, we should be going if we want to stay on schedule."

"Who are you, a German train engineer or something? Give them a second, for crying out loud."

I grin widely at my best friend for standing up for me and know in that moment that everything is going to be go great.

As we pull apart, I hear two sets of feet running towards us and Danielle's sharp inhale. "What the hell happened to you two?!"

"*Oh, shit*," Vinny mutters under his breath. "I'm gonna need another drink."

Frowning, I turn towards the commotion and watch as my niece and nephew run towards me with huge smiles on their faces. "Wow, Auntie Liza! You look like a Princess."

Before I have a second to really notice anything, I smile and bend at the knees, outstretching my arms to pull them into a hug just when I hear everyone collectively yell, "*No!*"

Immediately after pulling both kids into a group hug, their parents start to peel them forcefully off. Vinny looks down at me, his face pale and full of concern, while Danielle is so red and enraged she looks like she's about to blow a gasket.

"What the *hell* did you do, Vincenzo Castelli?"

I watch as everyone stares at me in horror, so I stand up straight, frowning. "What? What is it?"

Unfortunately, no one seems to be able to give me an answer. All they're able to do is stare at me, utterly mute. Rosie covers her face with her hands and groans, her eyes full of pity, while Barbara's slack-jacked.

"Why are you all looking at me like that?"

But no one dares say anything.

"*Fuck.*" Vinny mutters.

"Fuck! Fuck!" The twins start singing, trying to jump up and down in place as their parents try to hold them still by the shoulders. It's only then that I notice it. I notice the brown stains all over the twins' clothes.

No. No no no no.

NO.

Finally, I turn to my mother. "*Ma?*"

"It seems—" She clears her throat, her brows furrowed. "It seems the twins must have been playing outside in the mud. And... well." She waves her hand up and down my body. Bracing myself for what I might find, I look down and gasp in horror.

"Oh my god."

I'm only now processing the fact that my dress is covered in mud when I catch John barreling down the hallway towards us, eyes wide with panic. Breathless, he stops a few feet away from us and eyes each of us with hesitation, as if not knowing how to approach us.

"We're dealing with a crisis here, John. Can you give us a minute?" Danielle asks, her tone firm and commanding.

John sighs in relief, hunching over and supporting himself by placing his hands on his knees. "Oh, good. So you heard. I was scared I was going to have to be the one to give you the bad news."

"That Liza's dress is ruined?" Barbara asks, annoyed. She rolls her eyes and turns away from him. "Like we couldn't all notice, thank you." Then, in a low voice: "This guy. I mean, seriously?" She throws a thumb over her shoulder and shakes her head.

"Oh, no. That's not what I meant."

We all turn to face him again, feeling a chill run down my spine as my eyes meet his. "What other bad news are you talking about, then?" I ask slowly, bracing myself.

"Okay, well." He scratches the back of his head and looks down at his feet. "There seems to have been an issue with the caterers, apparently."

"*What* issue?" My mother's voice is venomous as her hands go to her hips. She's a small lady, but her expression is so deadly, John recoils.

"Um, well." He laughs once, uncomfortably. "They're not coming."

Chapter Four

MATT

I fidget with my cufflinks again, straightening my sleeves under my jacket, shifting my weight impatiently from one foot to the other as I stare towards the end of the aisle, waiting for Liza to walk down it.

"Matt, dude. Will you stop? You're making *me* anxious, and I'm not even the one getting married," Guru, one of my groomsmen, whispers in my ear, making me jump a little.

I meet his gaze and nod seriously, trying to contain this weird feeling coursing through me. This good kind of electric anxiety, of anticipation, of finally—*fucking finally*—getting to marry my girl.

He places a hand on my shoulder, shaking me a little. "You good?"

Am I good? I want to laugh at the question. At how ridiculous the assumption of me "not being good" is right now.

I don't think anyone's ever been this happy.

Patting him on the back, I whisper back, "Yeah, no. I'm good. Thanks, man."

I look around at all the friends and family who joined us for this special moment; at the arch above me under which we'll be married. I look around at the beautiful kaleidoscope of oranges, warm yellows, dark greens, and browns surrounding us. At the terracotta leaves blowing in the air all around us, the white pumpkins lining the aisle my future wife will walk down in just a few minutes and marvel at the significance of this very moment.

This life with Liza... It's nowhere near anything I could've ever possibly dreamed of. Life with her is so much more than I ever could've hoped.

It's been almost two years since being here with her first, walking these very grounds, eating apple cider donuts and flirting, and falling in love "at second sight," as she likes to call it. Almost two years of love and sex and lazy Sunday mornings in bed together. Of *family*—the true meaning of it, something I feel I haven't had since I was a teenager. Without her, I wouldn't have my daughter—my favorite person in the world. I wouldn't have family lunches, a strong support system. So much love.

Life has been better than good to me in the past couple of years.

If there's one thing I could change—*one thing*—it would be the traumatic experience of Lucy's birth. Of the hours of labor Liza was in—thirty-six—of the pints of blood she lost and of the sheer terror I felt at the thought of not just losing her, but at one point, Lucy, too.

If I couldn't even imagine the pain of losing Liza then, of the possibility of living in a world without her, I didn't even want to entertain the idea of what it would feel like to lose my daughter as well.

I squeeze my eyes shut and shake my head, not wanting to think about that moment again; not wanting to sully *this* moment with that traumatic one. Instead, I try to focus on the good parts, on reframing the memory of my daughter's birth. I try to focus on when I got to hold her in my hands for the first time and how I would never have expected the overwhelming feeling of joy and just... *wholeness* I felt in that one moment. I try to focus on seeing my future-wife holding our child, the look in her eyes as she cooed gently, beaming down at our daughter. How, even after everything she had been through physically and psychologically—after all the pain and the exhaustion—Liza could still be so strong and stay awake for a few more hours after that.

I've heard that some people find it difficult to look at their partners as more than just the mother of their child after giving birth, but it had the opposite effect on me. Seeing her like that— loving, nurturing, but also like she would kill anyone who dared mess with her family—made me want her even more. How could I not? I love her and she's given me the most incredible gift she could ever give me. But she's been off-limits for a while, and it's been extremely hard. *Literally.*

All that ends tonight.

I smile to myself, looking down at my feet, running the back of my hand over my mouth to hide the shit-eating grin spreading across my face at just the thought of being with her today after so long.

It's been a month of torture, of being so fucking in love with her and wanting to be with her and not being able to show her just how much. Of feeling her in bed, pulling her close, my nose in her hair, and having to control myself. Of storing every single thing I want to do to her in my mind for the minute—no, the *second* we're able to get physical again.

The thought alone makes my pants start to feel a little snug and I stifle a frustrated groan, trying to get a hold of myself. I'm getting married in a couple of minutes, for Christ's sake! I can't... *be* like this when it happens.

I sigh and run my fingers through my hair, impatient. I just want this over with. I want this to be done and official and over with.

I check my watch again—the one that used to belong to my dad—and see that we're behind schedule. *Fifteen minutes* behind schedule. Isn't that a little too late? What's going on? Where's Liza?

I take a deep breath and try to settle myself, my hands fidgeting with my cufflinks again.

Suddenly, I see my future-mother-in-law power-walking towards me with a frown on her face, holding the skirt of her blue dress in her hands so as not to trip, furtively glancing at the people seated on either end of the aisle.

My stomach drops and I feel a sudden knot in my throat.

What the hell is happening?

Liza wouldn't bail, would she? No. Of course not. That's ridiculous. She loves me. I know she loves me. She wouldn't do that to me. Plus, we have a child together.

Stop it, Matt. You're being ridiculous.

When Catterina finally reaches me, I know something's gone horribly wrong. I do my best to swallow the knot in my throat before asking, "What happened?"

She looks up at me with pity, and for half a second, I truly believe Liza's left. But then...

No.

"She won't come out. She's, uh—She's crying," Catterina whispers back.

"*What?*" My blood runs cold.

"She—"

I take off in the direction of the farm's main building without another word, leaving Catterina behind. My heart beats wildly against my chest as I run as fast as I can in these stupid dress shoes, trying not to slip in the mud and break my neck at the same time.

I burst through the front of the building and tear my way through it, headed straight for John's office, where I know it's been turned into the bridal dressing room.

I hear voices coming from it, its door ajar. *"Sweetie, it's fine. No one's going to notice anything. It's just a stain. You can barely see it."*

A freaking stain.

She doesn't want to come out because her dress is ruined?

This is insane.

"Just a stain?" I hear her wail. *"It's not just a stain. Look at me!"*

I take a minute to catch my breath before busting into that room and yelling at my fiancée for very nearly giving me a heart attack. But then... a sob. I straighten, my heart races again. *"It's not just that. It's everything."*

Not being able to hold back one second longer, I open the door, my eyes frantically searching for my future wife.

I find her sitting in an arm chair, tear-streaked, her dress somehow covered in mud at her waist, and sobbing—but still so fucking beautiful it takes my breath away. She gasps when she sees me and covers her face. "What the hell are you doing here? Don't you know it's bad luck to see the bride before the wedding?"

"Well," I clear my throat. "It seems like we're already having a bout of bad luck, aren't we? So why does it matter? I don't know if you know this, but we're supposed to be getting married today." She looks up at me and grimaces, looking repentant.

"Actually," I pause to check my watch, "we *were* supposed to get married about twenty minutes ago."

She uncovers her face and her bottom lip trembles, her wide eyes sad. "I know. I'm sorry," she says in a small voice. "I just—I just—" Her lower lip trembles and tears keep streaming down her cheeks. I kneel in front of her and cup her face, wiping the tears under her eyes with my thumbs as she bursts out crying again.

"Talk to me," I plead.

She closes her eyes and shakes her head. "Everything's ruined. My dress, the food... And now I started crying and I can't stop and we should've gotten married in City Hall and avoided this whole mess and gone to lunch to our favorite burger place or whatever after. And now—"

"Okay, stop. Breathe. Please." I lean over and kiss the tip of her nose, feeling her loop her arms around my neck as if needing to hold on. I place my hands on her hips and pull her closer to the edge of her seat.

"It's stupid, but I got so overwhelmed and now there's no food to serve the guests and my dress is horrible and I don't know what to do," she mutters into my neck. "And I really, really, *really* miss my dad," she whispers low in my ear, the pain in her voice so clear it slices through me.

My arms tighten around her, holding her as close to me as possible without crushing her lungs. And even though I feel her pain because I also lost my dad and would love to have him by my side today, her pain is a little different from mine. Sure, she has Vinny to walk her down the aisle, but I know she obviously would've given anything for her dad to be the one to do it.

I pull away from her and kiss her on the forehead before looking her in the eye. I can't do anything about Pietro not being here, unfortunately, but I might be able to help with the other stuff.

"How badly is the dress ruined? Can't you just dab it clean or something?" The death stare I receive from all the women in the room in return for my comment is nothing short of terrifying.

"No, I cannot just *dab* it off," Liza slightly raises her voice, rubbing her fingers under her eyes. "I can't wear this, Matt."

I could lie to her and tell her you can't really notice it, but she'll likely kill me, because it's obviously not true. "Don't you have another dress you could wear, maybe?"

If looks could kill, I'd have been murdered by all five women for that comment for the second time today. Apparently, that wasn't the right thing to say either.

"Matt, honey," Danielle patronizingly pats me on the shoulder. "This isn't like bringing a spare shirt in case you get food on it or something."

I glare at her, because I *know* that. I was just making a suggestion based on *logic. Given the situation, can't she just wear any old dress?*

But at this point, I know better than to press on that. Apparently, there's no room for logic when it comes to weddings.

Wanting to move on from the topic of the dress, I ask, "What happened to the food? I thought part of the deal was that the farm had this partnership with a restaurant here and they'd do our catering? I mean, I remember there was a tasting." I think back to the amazing selection we'd picked out for our wedding. Liza had been dreaming about their butternut squash soup for weeks, but I'd been craving the incredible steak. My mouth immediately waters, and only then do I realize just how hungry I am. I haven't eaten anything all day because of the nerves. "What happened to everything we picked out?"

Liza looks to someone behind me, and I follow her gaze. John meets my gaze with some hesitation, with something akin to terror, and takes an almost instinctual step back. "I'm really sorry, man. This was our first wedding and I guess I got things mixed up. Of course I'll refund you the money—"

"What do you mean you got things 'mixed up'? What. Happened?" I ask again, an edge to my voice this time.

Danielle steps in, arms crossed in front of her chest. "He booked the caterers for *next year.*"

"*What?*" I gawk.

"I'm *really* sorry, man." John takes a step back, terrified.

"See?" Liza wails again. "I *told* you. Everything is a mess." She sniffs and wipes her nose with the back of her hand. "God, I'm so weepy. It's so silly, but I guess I didn't realize just how much I really wanted this wedding. At first, I was doing it mostly for you, but somewhere along the way, I guess I got more into it than I thought I would... And now..." Another sob. "This is so stupid. I shouldn't be crying this much. It just sucks that we have to send everyone home and postpone and—"

"*Postpone?* What the hell are you talking about?" I frown and take her hands in mine, squeezing them lightly. There's no way I'm delaying this any further. "Hey. We'll figure something out. I promise. We can save this."

"Matt. Come *on*." She stares up at me with a sad, resigned look in her eyes. "We have a bunch of guests waiting outside, and they're expecting a wedding with food and a bride that doesn't look like a swamp monster," she says.

"You do not look like a swamp monster," I practically growl. Who gives a shit if her dress is ruined? It doesn't take away from the fact that she's never looked more beautiful.

"You know what I mean." She sniffs once and wipes her face, pushing her hair behind her ear.

I squeeze my eyes shut and pinch the bridge of my nose, trying to think up ways to make this right. Suddenly, I sit up, a grin spreading across my face. "I know what to do."

Chapter Five

MATT

"Honestly, I don't think there's anything you can do at this point. Not in the next five minutes, anyway."

I laugh once and shrug. "Probably not the next five minutes, but give me forty-five-ish?"

Liza's eyes widen with disbelief. I don't blame her, but we need a Hail Mary here.

"You're crazy. Absolutely insane. There is no way we can salvage this situation, unless you think I'm getting married in leggings and we're hitting the drive-through for every single one of our guests." She crosses her arms in front of her chest, her brown eyes on mine.

"Not drive-through, no." I wince. "But... maybe this could work by having a barbecue?" I ask hesitantly.

Her jaw drops, eyes widening. "A *barbecue*? What do you mean 'having a barbecue'?"

I scoot closer to her, taking her hands in mine again. "Okay, hear me out. I know we went through all the stressful wedding planning and all in a short amount of time and how I guess it seems now like it was all for nothing—"

"*So* much time and stress wasted on planning this thing."

"—but we can do this. I mean, remember how you wanted to just go down to City Hall and then head out to our favorite burger place? Make it super chill?" She nods, a faint glow of hope in her eyes. "Well, now we can do both—have the best of both worlds. Sure, it's not the delicious food we were planning on, but *fuck* if a burger doesn't sound amazing right now, too." She smiles at that, her face lighting up a little. "And the guests will understand, given that we only invited our closest friends and family. It's not like we have to put on a show for anyone. So who cares? Let's do it."

I watch as her expression shifts; she closes her mouth and eyes me with what I can only describe as skeptical optimism.

"*A barbecue?*"

"Yeah," I nod, going through the logistics in my head, suddenly feeling more and more confident in my ability to pull this off with every passing second. "I'm sure John has a grill or two he can let us borrow, don't you, John?" I look over at the owner of the farm, eyes narrowed. He *better* cooperate as best as possible with us. "I mean, given that this particular issue is your fault, since you didn't confirm the dates with your caterer."

The entire room's gaze shifts to John and he physically recoils, face ashen. "Yeah, I—" He clears his throat, nerves betraying him. "I have a couple of big grills out back, but I don't know if they'll be enough—"

"Gas or charcoal?" I ask.

"Gas."

Perfect. Cuts the set-up time by a huge margin.

This just might work.

Vinny snorts at John and mutters, "Real men do charcoal," under his breath.

John's back straightens, and he looks down at Vinny, squaring his plaid-wearing chest and shoulders with newfound confidence. "Actually, kid. Real men don't have time to babysit a charcoal grill for hours, waiting for it to heat up enough to use. We've got work to do. Gas grills are what *real* men use, thank you very much."

Liza breaks a smile, and I stifle my laughter, happy their little squabble has relieved some of the tension in the room. Vinny mumbles something under his breath and walks over to the cheese board, helping himself to generous amounts of it.

Redirecting the conversation, I say, "So, you have a couple of grills. Great. We can use those."

Liza looks up at me like I've lost my mind. "Matt. You can't be serious."

"Um," Barbara interrupts, raising her hand in the air like a kindergartner. "I think it'll be kind of cool. And Matt's right. How many people did you invite total? Like forty—maybe fifty guests? Shouldn't be awful. And it's all people you're close to, so it's not like it'll be a big deal, you know? Everything else in the wedding is perfect—besides your dress and the twins' clothes—so what does it matter whether the food is gourmet or not? It's whatever, in the grand scheme of things. We just want to see the both of you happy! Matt's right—there's no one to impress."

Liza snorts. "What about Matt's *boss*?"

"Please," I scoff. "Dr. Parker freaking loved you since the moment he met you. You're the reason I'm his favorite doctor in the practice, I think. He's not gonna care."

She smiles, taking my hand in hers. I see the hope starting to build within her and grin, because this can definitely work. We just need to work together.

I look around at the people in the room and start by assigning tasks. "Okay, cool. There's a mall about ten minutes away from here with a grocery store and a liquor store and *maybe* a craft store? I say we divide and conquer."

I get to my feet with determination, turning to face Vinny.

"You and I are going to head to the grocery store and buy every goddamn burger patty, hot dog, steak, buns, and chips that we can find."

Vinny swallows, eyes wide, and wipes his hands on his suit pant. "Aye, Aye, captain!"

"Barbara, did you and Theo bring a car?" She nods quickly, enthusiastically. "Great. You guys go to the liquor store. Take Rosie with you so she can check out the craft store and maybe find something that might help fix the dress?" I look over at Liza's new friend with a hopeful glance.

Rosie plays with a stray curl and looks over at Liza's dress with a desperate look in her eyes. "I don't think there's enough time to—"

"*Please*," I beg, bringing my hands together. I flash my eyes to my bride and Rosie nods. I don't care what she has to do—or if it even works, to be honest. I just need Liza to have some peace of mind; something to hold her together while we work to plan a wedding in less than an hour.

"Okay, I'll do my absolute best." Rosie places a hand on Liza's shoulder and smiles down at her.

"What about dessert?" Catterina interrupts. "And plates and cups?"

"I'll—" John clears his throat. "I'll provide you guys with the desserts. Our souvenir shop is filled with apple cider donuts and pumpkin loaf we just baked for tomorrow. We also have cider, so..." he trails off, his eyes on Rosie. "The farm will put that up since this was, uh, our mistake."

"*Your* mistake, you mean." Danielle crosses her arms in front of her chest and glares at him.

"Yes. And, uh... Well, we were the ones providing the plates and cutlery and stuff, so that's fine. The tables are set and everything. No need to worry about that. And of course, the florists were here this morning, so we're good there, as well."

"Perfect." I clap my hands together, pumped. We can do this. I know we can. I am going to marry this girl today if it's the last thing I do, and if this is what needs to be done, then it will be done.

"What about us?" Danielle asks. "What should we do?"

"Danielle, you deal with the twins." I look over at them as they stare around at the adults with awe in their eyes. "Do they have a change of clothes or something?"

"They're little devils passing themselves off as toddlers." She rolls her eyes and puts her hands on her hips. "Of course I do."

"Great." Feeling victorious, I smile down at my girl.

I walk over to my beautiful daughter, who has been napping in her Pack-n-Play through all this madness. With a smile on my lips, I resist the urge to pick Lucy up, even if it's just for a moment. Risking her waking up and having a tantrum now is absolutely not what Liza needs right now. "And I'll ask my mom and her husband to help with the guests."

I turn to face Liza again. "See? We got this."

"And I don't have a task?" She asks.

"You have the most important task ever. You have to—"

"If you say something stupid like my task is to 'just relax' I'm going to—"

"—just relax, babe." I smirk at her annoyed expression.

"I want to help," she pouts.

"I know, baby, but I don't want you to. I want you to calm down and eat some cheese and spend some time with our girl and just chill here, okay?"

Danielle puts her hands on her hips and grins. "You know, I always knew you'd be amazing for her. That's why I went to bat for you with Vinny last year."

"Oh, come *on*. I wasn't that bad, you guys." My best friend and brother-in-law rolls his eyes, as if he didn't try to beat me to a pulp in his childhood kitchen two Thanksgivings ago.

I ignore his comment and walk back to Liza, cupping her face with my hand and placing a kiss on her forehead. "So, what do you think? Are you okay with this new version of our wedding?"

Liza inhales sharply and smiles broadly up at me, squeezing my hand. "Yeah. I mean, it sounds like it would actually work. And honestly, the way I'm feeling now, I'd rather have a cheeseburger than some fancy crab cake or whatever." I can practically feel Catterina wince at the word '*cheeseburger*,' but this wedding isn't about her, so she doesn't press.

"It's complete madness, though. I mean, I thought planning a wedding in three months was bad, but in forty-five minutes? Seems kind of crazy. We could also wait a few months—or even a year—and just have a conventional wedding." She shrugs, playing it off like it's fine, but I know she wants this as much as I do.

I kneel down in front of Liza again and press my forehead against hers. "So far, *nothing* in our relationship has been conventional. Why start now?" I chuckle.

Her smile is bright and wide as she looks up at me. "You're amazing. Thank you," she breathes, her chocolate-brown eyes almost hypnotizing.

Filled with the overwhelming emotion that comes with knowing that soon we'll be married, I press my lips to hers. But what was intended to be a chaste kiss quickly turns heated as her fingers dig into my hair, pulling me closer into her. Immediately, my breathing speeds and my heart begins to race, all the blood from my body going straight to my cock. And we're back to what it was before—to what it's always been like since that first day two years ago, here at this very farm.

Like fire to tinder.

Liza's fingers fist in my hair and I grunt, scooting closer into her, inhaling the sweet scent of her hair. My hand squeezes her thigh once before sliding it up her leg, over her hip, her waist. I stop right at her ribs, just below her breasts, where I rub my thumb just underneath, teasing, feeling the lace beneath my fingertip.

A small whimper against my mouth and suddenly, it takes everything in me not to drag her into a private room somewhere and rip this stupid fucking dress off her.

Jesus fucking Christ, I'm in a room full of people and I'm five seconds away from getting a full-on boner.

Ah, who am I kidding? I'm already there.

It's been a while.

A throat clears—very loudly—in the background, and I hear a disgusted groan from Vinny. "Can you guys stop that? It's fucking gross."

Liza pulls back—but not before tugging on my lower lip with her teeth, her eyes low-lidded and locked with mine.

With a smirk and a knowing look (and really intense beard-burn) she sits back comfortably in her chair and reaches out to cup my face with her hands. "Thank you."

And with that, off we go, each one of us to complete our tasks.

Chapter Six

MATT

O kay, so I may have miscalculated how easy this whole thing was going to be. Sure, in theory, the plan is quite simple: divide and conquer. Each one of us has an assigned a task, and we have to complete it within the allotted time—which should be enough. But even though the others—Vinny, Rosie, Barbara, and Theo—all seem to know what they're supposed to be doing, they keep veering off track.

And it's taking everything I've got left in me to not lose it on them.

Barbara wants to get creative with the drinks, searching for "one-hour bartenders" in Long Island, insisting "It's a thing". "How else do you think celebrities host spontaneous parties out here, Matt?" she says, not even looking up from her phone screen while we discuss the final game plan in the mall parking lot.

"Barbara, I don't care. Just get a couple of bottles of white and red wine and some vodka from the liquor store. I don't fucking know." I exhale and dig my fingers through my hair, on edge. I need to remind myself to calm down, to keep it together for Liza's sake. I am not going to let this delay us getting married. I just won't. But I also want to make it good for her. I don't want her looking back at today a few years down the line and thinking how she would've rather waited or not had any celebration at all...

Rosie pulls at my arm, trying to get my attention. "Honestly, Matt. I didn't want to say anything back there in front of Liza, but I don't think there's much I can do for her dress in such a short amount of time. And covering it with some random fabric won't—"

I take a deep breath, trying to block out the stress and enter into a temporary meditative state. A short one—just a few seconds—but enough that I can gather myself—get centered—instead of losing my mind. I know it's odd for a doctor to believe in holistic approaches to medicine, but it's been proven time and time again to reduce stress, which is bad for the heart. As a cardiologist, I can't really ignore that evidence—so I meditate often.

Right now, I try to visualize what I want. I try to visualize Liza walking down that aisle towards me, just minutes from being mine. I try to visualize tonight when I finally get to have her again after so long. How I'm going to take it slow with her, savor her—the *second* time around. The first time, however, there's no way I'll go slow or stay in control. The first time we're together as husband and wife, I'm going to—

I stop myself before I let my mind go too far down the gutter.

Soon.

"Rosie," I say, putting my hands on her shoulders. "This is your area of expertise. Do what you gotta do. All I care about is that get this dress to the point where my future wife feels comfortable enough to get married in it."

She nods once, a frown on her face.

"I have to go buy the food with Vinny now." The exasperation building beneath my skin is clear in my voice as I walk away in the direction of the grocery store. But as I put more and more feet between me and my friends, I realize my best man isn't following me. I look over my shoulder and find Vinny laughing at something on Theo's phone screen, completely at ease.

Is he kidding me?

"*Vinny!* We need to get going. Jesus-fucking-Christ! And Barbara, you and Theo need to stop trying to find a bartender, and go to the damn liquor store!"

I mean, seriously. Aren't things hard enough as it is right now?

Vinny rolls his eyes, but abandons whatever the hell was on Theo's phone screen.

"Jesus, I know we're all stressed bro, but no need to be *Groomzilla*. We've got you—I promise."

I shoot Theo a glare before pleading with him: "Just please buy the damn drinks, man. I'm begging you. I just want this to work out."

He comes over and slaps me on the back, smiling at me. "Don't worry, man. It's going to be great. I promise that by the end of today, you'll be *Doctor Married*, alright?"

I snort before turning back to the store, effectively leaving them behind, praying to God they get it together and help me achieve this near-impossible task.

I PINCH THE BRIDGE OF MY NOSE, SQUEEZING MY EYES shut. "Murder is a capital offense. You don't want to go to prison. Murder is a capital offense. You don't want to go to prison. Murder is a capital offense. You don't want to go to prison. Murder is a capital offense. You don't want to go to prison." I repeat that to myself under my breath over and over again as I watch Vinny pull things we don't need from the shelves, hopping on one of the three shopping carts we're driving and rolling away on it while squealing *"Wee!"*

I check the time on my watch, and take the cart from his hands. "Okay, *enough.* I think we're good."

He smiles at me, a little winded from his adventure. "Let's check the list, shall we?"

We go one by one down the neon pink Post-It we scribbled on right before leaving the farm and tick off each item on the list. "We've got everything," I say, feeling myself relax a bit in relief. "And a few things we didn't need, but that's fine."

We check out as quickly as possible while receiving a lot of odd looks from patrons and employees. I mean, how often do you see two men in suits with boutonnieres speed-shop through the grocery store, buying enough food to feed an army? Our cashier shoots us a glare from some reason, but I smile at her. "We're having a get-together."

Vinny rips open a bag of chips and snorts before shoving a fistful into his mouth. "Yeah, just a couple of people. *Small"*

The cashier—*Brandi,* according to her name-tag—rolls her eyes at us as we hustle to bag all the food and get out as fast as possible. I grimace at the total amount, signing up for a club card to this grocery store just to get the discount, and rush out to the car to load the trunk with Vinny.

Just as my future brother-in-law heads out to return the carts to their location, Barbara and Theo come out—*empty-handed.*

"No." I shake my head viciously, my eyes widening. "No. Not today. *Please.* Not today. I just want to make this day as perfect as possible for her given the circumstances. And it's so far from it right now that I'm legitimately scared she'll choose to just cancel the wedding altogether. And you showing up empty-handed is telling me that you did not, in fact, purchase all the liquor on the list I gave you and you did not listen to me. I love your crazy ideas, Barbara. I swear. But today isn't the day to go out and try something new." I groan and put my face in my hands. "Barbara, *please* tell me why you did this."

"Easy, Matt. You need to chill."

Theo puts a hand on Barbara's lower back and whispers, "Babe, maybe it's best not to tell Matt to chill right now."

Smart man.

She rolls her eyes and pats his chest before turning back to me. "Matt, you didn't even let me explain myself. We spoke to the liquor store owner, and it turns out his son and his buddies are these amazing bartenders. But they're out of work right now, so they offered to help out—for a price, of course."

I eye her suspiciously. "If these bartenders are so amazing, why aren't they currently at their jobs?"

"Well, *Matt.*" She puts her hands on her hips and glares back. "If you must know, this whole area is seasonal and a lot of things close up in the fall and winter, which is why they're currently unemployed. We're lucky the owner was so sweet and helpful. He called them up and they're on their way now to pick up the drinks from the store and take it back to the farm where they'll take over the beverage service, okay?"

I look over at Theo to confirm, and he nods once. "Seriously. She even got the owner to give us a discount on all the liquor and managed to get them to move quickly." He looks down at her with a proud smile on his face and kisses the top of her head. Barbara, to my surprise, blushes like a schoolgirl.

"Turns out, he and his wife are fans of *Celebrity Dance Battle* and loved watching me and Theo dance on the show. Plus, their kids grew up watching *Phantom Fighters.*"

Still remaining cautiously optimistic, I thank God Barbara is a former child star.

I weed through everything they've just said and try to focus on the important part: "Okay, so not a disaster?"

"*Ugh.* No, okay? I would never do that to my best friend. Are you kidding me? I want this day to be as special for her as you want it to be."

Doubtful, but I don't argue. No time, anyway.

"Fine, whatever," I wave a hand, trying to dismiss this problem so I can move on to the next one. The food is a bigger deal anyway, and I've solved that. "Where's Rosie?"

"Here!" We turn to face Rosie as she struggles to jog up from behind us in high heels, holding the skirt of her pink dress in her hands. "I'm here!"

I stare at her, slack-jawed. "You're—You're also empty-handed."

I check my watch and frown. It's been over forty-five minutes and she has nothing. Unless she also called someone who's on their way to fix or something, like Barbara and Theo.

"Before you freak out,"—she raises both hands in the air, stopping me—"just know that there's no way I was going to find anything acceptable there. I tried, but I promise nothing was going to work." I groan and grit my teeth. "But I *do* have a solution that won't take much. All I need is some help from you."

Chapter Seven

LIZA

"You've lost your mind, you know that? You want me to wear *that*?" I point at the white men's shirt being held up by Rosie. "You—Rosie Castillo, fashion queen—wants me to wear that shirt over it and cover the back of my dress up?"

She sighs, defeated. "I know it will hide the back and all the intricate beading and the amazing detail, okay? *I know*. But I also know you need to get married in, like, five minutes and we don't have many other options. Also, you can take it off after the ceremony to show off the beautiful back if you want—stains and all. Or for when you're all alone with Matt," she smirks. "Plus, it will keep you warm, since temperatures have dropped in the past hour and you're gonna end up freezing."

I eye the shirt again, hesitant. "Well, if I'm wearing Matt's shirt, what the hell is he going to wear?"

She exhales, rolling her eyes. "This is his spare. *Duh.*" I look down at my waist and grimace, taking in the mud stains. "So you just want me to wear this oversized shirt?"

"Yeah. I mean, it's obviously not going to look as beautiful as the dress by itself, but honestly, I think it'll look super cute. Especially since it's Matt's shirt. We'll roll up the sleeves and tie it around your waist, unbuttoning the top few buttons to reveal a little cleavage and the hint of the dress."

I stare at myself in the reflection and visualize it, not hating the idea. It's definitely better than ruining it by buying some material that doesn't match from a craft store or covering it in another way with whatever Rosie would've been able to find there.

"Honestly, you don't really have a choice. It's this, or you walk down the aisle with brown stains all over your beautiful dress."

I exhale heavily, scratching at the dry mud on my dress. When that (obviously) doesn't work, I reach out for the shirt and say, "Okay, give it to me."

She hands me Matt's shirt, and I'm suddenly hit with a wave of his scent. I bring the shirt to my face, careful not to get any makeup on the fabric, and inhale deeply, closing my eyes and letting it reach the corners of my anxious body. With every second, I feel every tight muscle begin to loosen as I remind myself of what's *really* happening today: I'm marrying Matt.

Everything else is just noise.

Suddenly, I feel like the world's biggest idiot. What does it matter what I'm wearing or what the food will be? Sure, being upset about all of this is reasonable, but hating this day or wanting to reschedule it is definitely not something I want. Getting married might not seem like something that's pressing given our situation, but it's something we both want.

Immediately, I feel like an ass for not being more excited about Matt's Plan B. He was just trying to do anything he could to make this possible today. *He* realized what was *really* important before I did: what's important is that, by the end of this day, Matt and I will be married—and it doesn't matter how.

When we first got engaged, I promised myself I wouldn't be Bridezilla or get super stressed about planning this whole thing. But it's so hard to not get caught up in the whole process, to not let yourself get roped into the stress of it all, and to maintain perspective on things.

So with another hit from Matt's scent coming off the fabric and this obvious realization in my mind, I slip my arms through the crisp white sleeves and begin to button the shirt. Rosie runs over to me, lightly slapping my hands away, whispering, "I got it."

When she's done rolling up the sleeves and tying it stylishly at my waist, I look at myself in the mirror and gasp. "Holy cannoli."

"I told you," she smiles proudly at my reflection, popping the collar of his shirt a little more. "Sure, it hides your sexy back, but it also perfectly hides the mud stains. And see how you can still see the beautiful fabric details from your sleeves? And it's not like the dress has a lot of cleavage, so you're not hiding anything there either. Plus, now you look like you just came out of a runway or something—that material under the shirt looks incredible."

And she's right. Somehow, she grabbed my future-husband's shirt and turned my beautiful fairy-like dress into something out of *Project Runway* or whatever. "Minimal effort, maximum style," she says, with a proud smile.

I reach out to grab her hand and squeeze it. "Thank you. This is perfect."

"It's not a big deal," she shrugs, grinning.

"No, it is. You helped earlier today with the buttons and now this and... Well, I'm so happy to have met you, Rosie. Really. Thank you." After everything today, I regret not having made her a bridesmaid. "This is awkward, but... when we were setting up our wedding party, you and I weren't really that close.

But I feel like we've come together since then, right?" I bite my lip.

"I—" She clears her throat. "Yeah."

Jesus, why is it so damn difficult to make new friends as an adult? Everything ends up sounding super awkward.

"Well, anyway. I was wondering whether you'd like to be a bridesmaid? I just—" I blow a gust of air. "It's more than last minute; it's last *second*. But then again, this entire wedding has been the same way. And you've become such a big part of our lives and really helped out today and during the planning process. I'd love it if you were officially part of this day."

She grins broadly and nods. "Yeah, okay. I'd love that." She squeezes my hand back, and after a moment says, "Well, now you're ready to get married."

I inhale sharply, turning to look at myself one last time in the mirror. "I've *been* ready for quite some time. Let's freaking do this."

ROSIE STRAIGHTENS MY TRAIN ONE MORE TIME, WHILE Barbara hands me my bouquet—a mix of sunflowers, dahlias, garden roses, and gerberas, all in the most beautiful autumnal colors. Mom checks on Lucy, making sure she's wrapped up and warm as she slumbers through this entire chaos in her stroller. Danielle smooths out my hair, which is looking less fancy than it did before.

"Okay, ready?" John claps his hands, giving us an anxious look. I haven't asked about the food or drinks or anything, because at this point, I don't really care. But by the *smell* of it, there's a grill going somewhere. Plus, knowing Matt, I'm sure he found a way to fix things to the point where we could host our guests and have food and not make it look like it was planned in under an hour. He has that problem-solving gift about him. And though I more than appreciate the effort, after my big moment in the dressing room, I realize none of that matters—Matt and I and Lucy are what matters. Our family.

With that, I stand up straight, center my bouquet just at my waist, and link my arm through my brother's before saying, "I was born ready," with a smirk.

Vinny snorts and shakes his head, leading me to the back of the wedding line that's quickly formed ahead of me, where we'll wait as everyone makes their way down the aisle.

First up are the twins—Leo as the ring bearer, Clara as the flower girl. Danielle has successfully cleaned them up and changed them into another outfit. Matt's mother and her husband are second, followed closely behind by my mom and a knocked-out Lucy (seriously, how lucky are we to have a baby that can sleep through virtually anything?). I hear the guests collectively *aww* at my daughter, despite the fact that I'm sure no one can really see her from their seats considering how bundled up she is.

The nerves start to build and the need to get this over with, to finally do this, increases with each second that passes. I jiggle a little, impatient. "Do you need to pee or something?" Vinny whispers in my ear. "Because I'm sorry to say—you're gonna have to hold it."

I smile up at him and shake my head. "Nah. Just tired of waiting for this moment to happen. It hasn't been too long when you think of it, but it *feels* that way. Like it's been a long time coming."

He nods in understanding and shoots me a warm smile. "I get it. I was like this with Dani, too." He looks over at my sister-in-law with a wistful look in his eyes, startling me. "We both made the right choice here. Me with Danielle, and you with Matt, I mean. I'm glad you lied to me and snuck around behind my back."

Shocked, I nearly take a step back to take a better look at him. He's *never* said anything like this before. *"You are?"*

"I mean, look. This isn't the best time to discuss it, but you definitely could've done worse. And I want to believe that if you'd been grownups about it and come to talk to me before, I would've been okay with it. But we both know that's not true. I would've flat out said no." He shrugs. "So, yeah. I guess I *am* happy you snuck around."

I laugh while we watch as Danielle makes her way down the aisle right behind Barbara, my maid of honor, followed closely by Rosie. "Thanks, bro. Love you."

"Yeah, yeah. Whatever. Don't get weepy on me now." But he smiles down at me and pulls me closer into him.

Our laughter is cut short as the wedding march begins and my stomach turns in anticipation. "Oh my God," I whisper under my breath.

"Let's do this, just like we did in rehearsal last night."

Together, my big brother and I begin to walk down the aisle, but I nearly freeze once my eyes fall on Matt. My breathing speeds and I'm suddenly fighting the urge to run towards him—and thank god, since it would be impossible to do in these shoes. His gaze meets mine and his face breaks into a broad smile, just as wide as mine.

"Finally," I see him mouth, his eyes shining bright with excitement.

I laugh once and sniff, not realizing until that moment that I've been crying. Our eyes never leave each other as Vinny and I make the slow-paced trip all the way to the makeshift altar in the middle of the beautiful field, practically shaking. After what feels like an hour, I finally make it to Matt, where he awaits with a glowing smile on his face.

Vinny grabs my hand and puts it into Matt's, as is tradition, but not before whispering, "Don't fuck this up" at him. I glare at my brother, annoyed, thanking the universe he at least had the decency to say it low enough so only Matt and I could hear.

My future-husband on the other hand just laughs and mutters back, "I swear I'll do my best not to," just as Vinny moves to stand next to him in his other role as best man.

Almost smugly, Matt pulls me up to stand in front of him, cupping my face in his hands. For the second time today, he swipes the tears from under my eyes with his thumbs. This time around, though, they're tears of joy.

He places a kiss on my forehead and takes my hand in his, and the ceremony begins.

As the officiant begins to speak, I barely process any of the words, focusing only on the man in front of me. I know we're in a beautiful field, surrounded by our friends and family. I know that, above us, is a beautiful floral arch that took multiple days of emailing back and forth with the florists to design. And I know that everyone is watching, but there's really nothing that can hold my attention away from the gorgeous man standing in front of me. Nothing that can hold my focus away from him and how, every now and then, he squeezes my hands in his shaky ones, making me smile.

After some time, I get lost thinking of our life now and what it will look like in ten, twenty, thirty years. It's not until I feel Barbara nudge me in the back with a *"Liza, Jesus. It's your turn,"* that I'm forced to come back to the present.

"Huh?"

Matt chuckles and leans in closer, a sudden wave of his cologne hitting me like a ton of bricks, fogging my already-cloudy brain even more. "It's your turn to say you do."

"Oh," I laugh nervously. I'd gotten a little carried away in my daydreaming, looking ahead to tonight when we'd finally be alone, away from everyone. "I do," my voice breaks, but I can't bring myself to be even a little embarrassed.

After we finish exchanging our rings, Matt doesn't hesitate to wrap his arms around my waist, pulling me in a little closer than is appropriate in front of our guests—especially in this setting. His eyes never leave mine as we both anxiously wait for the ceremony to be over. And then, before the priest is even done telling him he may now kiss me, his lips are on mine, desperate and hungry. I dig my fingers into his hair and feel tears streak down my cheeks as I process the momentous piece of information that this man is now officially *mine*.

Chapter Eight

MATT

The first thing I want to do after the ceremony is to take Liza into one of the makeshift dressing rooms and basically have my way with her. I consider waiting until everyone is distracted enough so we can make a run for it and be alone together for at least a few minutes. But as soon as it's over, we're called by the photographers to take some family and couple pictures. After what seems like hours (but was probably only twenty minutes), we're finally done and "*allowed*" to go back and enjoy our party.

A falsehood, naturally, because we're constantly pulled in different directions by our mothers to "Go say hi to you cousin X. He came all the way from Florida!" Or "Did you thank Mr and Mrs So-and-so for their gift?"

I want to share this moment with my wife, with my daughter, and my close friends, but it's like our wedding isn't really about us enjoying it and celebrating the way we want. Like we have to fulfill these...*obligations* before we're even allowed to.

And I'm so wound up from today—from *last night*, too—I

just need to feel close to Liza. I need alone time. I want to know how she's doing after seeing her so stressed out and unhappy before the ceremony. Is she okay? Has she calmed down? I haven't even been able to really talk to her besides being able to whisper how incredibly beautiful she looks tonight as we walked to where the photographer wanted to shoot us. I want to make sure that she's not too disappointed with how things turned out.

We did our best to solve the whole catering issue, but there was really only so much we could do with what little time we had, and I don't want to disappoint Liza today. Though it seems like John and his team have been able to run with our new plan. It's not some fancy dinner, but honestly, the whole burgers thing ended up being a much better plan than I thought it would.

At least that's what I think. I certainly don't mind having a bacon cheeseburger for dinner at my wedding, but who knows...

After even more photos and a few minutes of mingling, it's finally time for the first dance. Funnily enough, if you'd asked me yesterday, I would've told you this was the part of the wedding I was least looking forward to, not being a huge dancer myself. But after a day like today, I can't think of anything better than getting some alone time with Liza, just holding her in my arms like this, moving to the rhythm of the music. I want to be able to speak privately and ask her how she's doing, and, at the rate we're going, it seems like it's the only way I'll be able to get it done.

"By the way," I whisper in her ear as soon as I have my arms around her, "it was a close call, but I'm pretty sure we're good on the whole food thing. By the looks of it, it John has a handle on everything now." I scan the room and watch the waitstaff serve people cheeseburgers and hotdogs with sides of coleslaw and pickles. Despite it being unconventional for a wedding, I haven't seen one disappointed look in the crowd—not even from my heart-conscious coworkers. I smile and watch as Guru tosses back a gin & tonic, smiling coyly at one of Liza's grad school friends. "Plus, it's kind of amazing, but Barbara managed to rope these guys she met through the liquor store owner into—" Liza leans back and places a finger to my lips, silencing me, smiling softly up at me.

"Matt. It's okay. It's all okay. Before, with the dress, the food... I was being silly." She closes her eyes and shakes her head. "None of it matters. Not really. Not enough for me to have been crying over it like that. What matters is this. *Us*. I'm sorry if I overreacted over the stupid dress and the food and—" She exhales deeply, the gold specks in her chocolate brown eyes vibrant and glowing under the rows of twinkles lights above us. "It's not the reason why we were getting married."

I frown. "I know. But your feelings were still valid, Liza. You had a right to be upset. Don't make yourself out to be a Bridezilla or something just because you were stressed about the fact that what we'd planned had suddenly all gone wrong." I kiss her nose, wanting to put her at ease. "Plus, it's a big, emotional day in general."

"Yeah... It's been difficult. I think I haven't missed Dad this much since I think the first year he was gone." She clears her throat and presses her face into her nook—where my shoulder and neck meet.

"I know what you mean. My dad and I had a much closer and special relationship than my mom and I had. So I really missed him today, too. But," I pull away to look her in the eyes. "I know that, even though you try to hide it, today was especially hard for you because he wasn't here to walk you down the aisle. Or have a father-daughter dance." Her mouth twists into a grimace, her eyes shining with unshed tears.

We're quiet for a moment while I just revel in the magic that is holding her to me, breathing her in, appreciating this for what it is.

She smiles sadly up at me for a minute and whispers, "Thank you, Matt. For being so amazing and understanding. For loving me the way that you do."

Our foreheads touch, and I smile down at her, out mouths barely an inch apart. "I don't know about being amazing, but I'll always try to be as understanding as possible. Always." I kiss her again.

"Mama! Papa!" Liza and I pull away from each other to turn to watch Lucy try to free herself from Catterina's grasp. The expression on our daughter's face is so comically tragic, I can't help but chuckle. With a nod, Liza signals to her mother to let our girl wobble over to us in her burgundy dress, brown tights, and party shoes. I squat down to catch her in my arms and settle her on my hip while she wraps her arms around my neck, monkey-style. With a huge smile on my face, I pull both my girls in and happily lead them on the dance floor. Together, we dance to the rest of The Rolling Stones' *Wild Horses* just like Liza and I did that first time in her apartment. I kiss my daughter on the cheek and then my wife, and marvel at all that's passed and everything that's to come.

WE FINISH OUR FIRST DANCE AS A FAMILY AND OUR GUESTS immediately join the dance floor, where the three of us continue to dance together for several songs. Eventually, though, Lucy gives up on us and cries for *Baba* (AKA, Barbara, her godmother), who happily takes her in her arms. Liza and I watch them for a bit before I pull my wife back in my arms, and we sway to the rhythm of the next song.

It isn't until a couple of minutes later that, for the first time since this hectic day began, no one is paying attention to us. Catterina, Theo, and Barbara are doting over my daughter as she *tries* to twirl gracefully in front of them; Danielle is running after her twins, while Vinny is too busy drunkenly doing the electric slide to notice; and my mother and step-father are deeply engrossed in a conversation with Dr. Parker. I look around and realize that every one of our guests is too busy having fun, eating and dancing, and no one—not one single person—is currently paying attention to the bride and groom.

Suddenly, a shot of excitement runs through me, and I take my wife's hand in mine. She looks up at me with a questioning look in her eyes, but I only reply by wiggling my eyebrows at her, a smirk on my face.

Liza throws her head back in laughter, understanding immediately what I'm trying to convey, and the sound of it knocks me breathless. But I don't let it distract me; we need to get out of here before anyone notices.

I take her hand and lead her off the dance floor, towards the back, completely avoiding the crowds and the tables. We sneak out of the barn through a side-door, looking back only once to make sure no one's followed us.

Giggling like a pair of kids, we run around out back and, once we're free and clear, I pull her into my arms and give her a plundering kiss, pushing her against the barn wall. I'm already almost painfully hard just from kissing her, my mind filling with filthy fantasies about how I plan to fuck her for the next forty-eight hours.

After a few minutes of intense making out, she puts her hands on my chest and pushes me slightly away. Panting, she asks, "Where are you taking me?" Her face is hopeful, chocolate brown eyes alive with need. I want to make a joke about taking her in more ways than one, but I stop suddenly, some overwhelming feeling making me speechless.

Liza looks up at me, concern clear on her eyes, and brings a hand to my cheeks. "Hey. Are you okay?" She frowns, eyes bouncing between both of mine.

I put my hand over hers, holding it to me. "We're *married*," I whisper intensely. My chest feels tight with this feeling of intense happiness—of pure *joy* that I've only ever felt with Liza and Lucy. I struggle to breathe while my mind continues to process this momentous piece of information.

"Oh, is that what that whole thing was about earlier today?" She smirks at me.

I snort and pull her hand to my lips, kissing the center of her palm before nipping at the tip of her index finger. She squeals a bit, but laughs.

"It's a good thing, though, right?" She asks, her voice suddenly insecure.

I balk at my new wife. "How can you even say that? Of course it's a good thing."

"I don't know your life," she teases, looking relieved. "You might've changed your mind."

"About us?" I scoff, wrapping my arms so tightly around her waist that I lift her a few inches from the ground. "Never." I sigh, dropping her gently back on her feet.

Liza loops her arms around my neck, pulling me down towards her. I close the space between us and kiss her, our lips immediately opening to each other, tongues exploring. It's not long before we're panting again, before Liza's fingers are fisted in my hair, before my hands start traveling all over her body and she's moaning in my mouth as I press my hips into her, letting her feel all of me.

"That's it," I growl, pulling away suddenly and grabbing her by the hand.

"Wha—?" But I turn to cut her off with a deep kiss before telling her, "I love you and I want you. So we're going somewhere where we can be alone together. *Now.*"

Chapter Nine

LIZA

I don't think I've ever seen Matt seem more... *eager*? More anxiously excited?

His breathing speeds and I can tell, even under his suit, that his muscles are tense with anticipation. I giggle as he leads me through the grounds, lit only by strings of twinkle lights, all the way to the main house.

Before opens the door, he turns to hold my face in his hands and gives me another deep, drugging kiss. The kind that turns my legs into Jello and clouds my mind—the kind that builds heat low in my belly and—

A low moan escapes my mouth, my fingers grasping at his jacket with impatience. I press myself closer to Matt, but he pulls away from me, looking down at me with wild eyes. After a beat, he pushes the door to the main house open, leading me to my dressing room, where we snicker like teenagers as he locks the door behind us.

From across the small room, we stare at each other for a moment, taking each other in.

Matt looks *delicious* in that suit, all broad-shouldered and tall—solid like an oak tree. His hair is rumpled from me running my hands through it, desperately wanting more, and his lips kiss-bruised from our hungry make-out-sesh. He looks like a total mess, and I *would* make a joke, but honestly I feel like my chin is on fire, which means that I have some pretty intense beard burn as well.

I laugh at what someone would think if they saw us now, at how disheveled and rumpled we must look. But I'm quickly interrupted by the hungry look in Matt's eyes as he slowly prowls towards me, green eyes darkened with need.

My breath hitches as his lips fall on mine once more and he walks me backwards against the wall, his hands on either side of me, caging me in.

"I love you," he whispers against my lips, his hand travel to my breast. "You've made me the happiest man alive. And I really, *really* want you. *Now*." Matt is such a sweet and caring man in general, but when it comes to sex... I love when he loses control—when he *takes* it.

Without further preamble, my hands fly up to his tie to loosen it and pull it off from around his neck. I push his jacket off his shoulders, feeling his strong muscles under my fingertips, and attack the buttons of his shirt while he kisses down my neck. His hands slide down to my hips, fingers digging into me through the fabric of my dress, desperate groans causing an electric current to run down my spine.

I do my best to control myself as his hand pulls my skirt up, heat and need building between my legs, his fingers gently graze my skin as they travel up and up and up to the junction of my thighs. But it's getting harder and harder to care about anything but the way he pushes me roughly against the wall, the way he groans when his fingers skim the fabric of my panties, how gravelly his voice sounds in my ear as he says, "You're so fucking *wet*".

I moan and throw my head back, hitting the wall with a loud thud as he starts to circle me just right. Losing all focus, I abandon my task of unbuttoning his shirt. I can barely catch my breath as I spiral quickly after a month of built up need, feeling my orgasm just *there*—so. Freaking. Close.

Feeling my body tense with anticipation, right on the edge, Matt pulls back with a smirk on his face, causing me to nearly fall over. "I know we need this to be relatively quick, but not *that* quick," he murmurs.

Matt laughs at my pout, but leans over to bite my lower lip, pressing himself against me. Of their own accord, my hips begin to move, seeking friction and release.

He feels so good.

"I don't want to come like this. Need you inside," I pant in his mouth.

Matt sucks on the delicate skin beneath my ear, my eyes rolling in the back of my head. "Then fucking undress me," he practically growls.

My hands fly to his buttons once more, shaking from the adrenaline coursing through my body. I need to remind myself constantly that, despite the fact that I want to rip his clothes off, we need to eventually get back to the party, and I'm wearing his only spare shirt. Thankfully, I make it to the last button before I completely lose all self-control, my skin tingling with anticipation. Matt, seeming to read my mind perfectly, grabs holds of my wrists and presses them above my head.

"Still," he orders, voice low and gravelly in my ear, raising goosebumps all over my skin. I inhale sharply at his command, at the feeling of his tongue over on me, and almost melt into a puddle at the rough, "Good girl," that follows.

Matt quickly takes his shirt off, tossing it aside somewhere over his shoulder. He helps me unknot mine and quickly pushes it off, letting it fall to our feet. The hunger in his eyes softens a bit as his eyes trail slowly up and down my body, taking in my wedding dress. "You're beautiful. This dress— " a sharp inhale as his eyes roam my body. His throat bobs as he swallows hard, his expression tender, though I can still see the need in his eyes. "You're so damn beautiful."

I grimace. "Nah. But I probably would've been closer to it if the dress weren't destroyed."

He shrugs, his smile crooked. His hand goes to cup my face, slides to the nape of my neck where his fingers dig into my hair. "Would've married you in leggings and that ratty old t-shirt you wear all the time, and I still would've thought you were the most beautiful bride. Because you are."

My heart warms in my chest, feeling a little bit like I could cry. "Make love to me," I whisper, fully aware that our surface options are very limited at the moment.

But I don't care. I don't care about the fact that we've snuck out of our own wedding party and that we've left all of our guests. I don't care that the first time that we'll have sex as husband and wife is going to be in a messy room in the main house of this pumpkin farm, while everyone will be wondering where we are. I don't care that all of our wedding plans went out the window and we had to plan a new one in under an hour.

None of that matter because—though I am one-hundred percent a feminist and independent and all of that—the idea that Matt is *mine* and I'm *his* has me so turned on I'm just a few seconds from begging him to rip this stupid dress off me and— Well. You get the picture.

He comes at me again, so desperate to get me out of his dress that he tries to slip my arms out of its sleeves without even trying to unbutton it first. "Buttons," I mumble against his lips. "The buttons on the back of the dress."

Impatiently, I turn around to face the wall, expecting him to get to work immediately on the short vertical row of small, silk covered buttons that trail from my lower back to my tail bone. But instead of feeling eager fingers unhook each and every one of the twelve buttons on my dress, I hear a soft groan from Matt, before he slams his right hand next to my face on the wall, dropping his head to my shoulder, breathing me in. "*Fuck.*" He exhales, his breathing a little ragged. I feel Matt's other hand hold me tightly around the waist as he presses his hip against me. I feel every inch of him—hard and ready. "*This* is what you had under my shirt? Thank God I didn't see it earlier. I would've jumped you during the ceremony. I probably wouldn't have been able to be much help consoling you and coming up with a Plan B after everything with the caterers went wrong. I would've struggled to restrain myself in front of everyone and taken you in this very room."

I snort, but all humor quickly dissolves from my body when he slowly trails his fingers down my spine, tracing patterns, my nipples tightening against the soft silk lining of my dress. Liquid heat builds between my legs as he bites into my neck from behind, and I moan, feeling empty, needing him to fill me.

The sound is like a starting pistol for Matt, who takes on the challenge of freeing me from my dress in less than ten seconds— no small feat, considering how delicate and difficult those tiny buttons are. He takes my hand and helps me step out of the puddle of tulle and lace, but not before taking a moment. He looks me over, head to toe, taking in my white pumps, white stockings, and white lace thong.

"*Jesus.*" He covers his mouth with his hand, his eyes wide as they travel over my body, my skin flushed with heat. "You're so —so—" But he doesn't manage to finish the sentence, opting instead to pull me roughly into him with a growl and pull me to the couch with him. He kisses me while we both clumsily work on his belt. I slap his hands away and pull his zipper down, tugging his pants and underwear all the way off with Matt's help.

I lean over to kiss him, my hand moving down his chest, making a path to take him in my hand. I wrap my hand around his cock, hard and ready and warm, and move my hand up and down a few times. Matt squeezes his eyes shut, mumbling nonsensical words, begging me to stop, telling me he's too close for this. Watching him squirm like this, wanting me, makes me ache even more. All of a sudden, Matt grabs me by the wrist, halting my movements. "No more. Please," he pants, grabbing me suddenly by the hips, dragging me on top of him.

I adjust my legs on either side of his, and roll my hips forward, feeling him under the delicate, wet lace in between my thighs. Matt squeezes his eyes shut and groans, digging his fingers into me.

Sitting on him like this, he holds me tightly and rocks me back and forth over him, the movement causing the liquid heat inside me to build, the need to feel him inside almost unbearable, and I'm gonna come, I'm going to—

"*Ah.*" I sit up, trying to control my breathing. Matt looks up at me with an expression that is half frustration, half concern.

"You okay?" He's breathless, eager to return to what we were doing.

But I need more.

I bend to take his lower lip in between my teeth. "Need you *inside* me."

His growl reverberates in his chest, eyes alight with hunger, with understanding. Matt's fingers travel to the apex of my thighs and he hooks my panties to the side, making room for himself.

I place a hand on his chest to balance myself on him, feeling his heartbeat beneath my fingertips, the quick-paced rhythm matching mine.

Suddenly, the almost-feral hunger for each other is replaced by the awareness of this near-seismic moment. We stare into each other's eyes, my forehead pressed against his, lips less than an inch apart, as I slide down on him.

The slow stretch is delicious, perfect, and just short of too much. I inhale sharply, feeling a shift between us in this moment, feeling a new level of closeness I thought Matt and I couldn't surpass at this point in our relationship. But whether it's the high of having just gotten married or really about the evolution of our relationship, I haven't even started moving and I already know it'll be the best sex of my life.

It's been so long, and he's so big, and though I'm more turned on than I think I ever have in my entire life, it's a little choppy at first, as my body gets used to him again. I can barely breathe as the pressure builds, at how tight it feels, at how delicious the friction feels, despite having to focus now on small movements.

Matt pants in my mouth, his brow covered in sweat, struggling to keep himself restrained and in control. But I want to feel him unleash himself, to give me everything, so I close my eyes, pressing myself into him as I bear down on.

We groan in unison, eyes squeezed shut as I call out his name, when he's buried himself to the hilt. Matt presses his lips against my ear, his breath rapid and uneven. "You're so beautiful," he tells me over and over again. He digs the fingers of his left hand into my hair, holding my head at the nape, and brings my face to his, kissing me so deeply I feel it in my toes. Matt wraps his other arm tightly around my waist, using it as leverage as he begins to piston into me from below.

My mouth breaks away from him in a gasp as I scream out his name. I dig my nails into his shoulders, trying desperately to hold on, but Matt's relentless. His mouth attacks my neck, the valley between my breasts, his tongue plays with my nipples, and he whispers dirty words against my damp skin that have me on the edge of bursting. "You're so wet and tight." He struggles to push the words out, almost gritting his feet. "I love you so much. I've been thinking of this for so long." His hand to travels between us, his thumb going to where we're connected and he touches me *there*, circling with enough pressure to make me almost lose my mind.

I see white spots behind my eyelids as I hear him whisper, "That's it, baby. Let go. Come with me."

He tightens his fist in my hair and brings my lips to his in a powerful, hard kiss, thrusting hard into me from below with a final, deep groan as he pulls me over the edge with him.

Epilogue

ROSIE

S*wipe left. Swipe left. Swipe—Oh, he's kinda cute.*

My thumb hovers over my screen as I take another look at the man in the photo—and zoom in on the dog in his arms instead. Classic dating app move to put a picture with an animal on your profile—but so transparent. The man holds no interest to me. None of the guys ever do. The *dog,* on the other hand...

I tinker briefly with the idea of getting a pet, but reconsider. My work hours are murder—there's no way I could give an animal the daily attention it deserves. The only way I could get one is if things settled down at work a bit. Maybe I could get a cat?

With a sigh, I lean my head on my hand, elbow on the table, and keep swiping away.

Left. Always left. Forever left.

Sometimes, on a rare occasion, I'll see someone who looks nice and normal and will force myself to swipe right. Of those, I'll *maybe* attempt to flirt a little, and very, *very* rarely, I'll actually meet them for a drink. Usually, though, it's a pathetic attempt on my end to find someone who I know will never measure up to the one person I want.

Still, don't I get points for trying? Even if it is only sometimes?

But as I chew on my thumbnail, eyes laser-focused on my phone screen, I realize that it's time I start pushing myself into actually getting to know some of these guys. After nearly a decade, I pretty much need to come to terms with the fact that the person I thought was the love of my life, just...isn't.

So I swipe right on the guy with the dog—a thinly veiled attempt to get women to find him more interesting—because, who knows? Maybe I'll get to play with it for the day if we go out on a date.

Immediately, my phone buzzes with a notification. We're a match, apparently. And not five seconds later Jake, 33, from Montauk, is messaging me, asking me to meet him in ten minutes for a drink somewhere close by.

So...no chance I'll be getting to see that dog, then.

"Agh." I dump my phone on the table and take a sip of my wine, frustrated with dating apps and over-eager single men and "getting drinks" and random dates. But mostly, I'm frustrated with myself. With my inability to let go. With the fact that I'm currently at my friend's wedding, supposed to be having fun, but am sitting alone at my table going through my phone instead.

I should be out on the dance floor, enjoying myself. I should be flirting with one of the cute single groomsmen—Matt's cute doctor friend, for example. Instead, I'm here pouting, thinking about the biggest mistake I ever made.

As I look around, my eyes fall on the back door near the band, where I watch a very disheveled Liza and Matt sneak their way back into the party. Amused, I watch as she adjusts his tie and finger-combs his hair back into place with a soft smile on her face. Matt looks down at her with a knowing smirk, as if no one can tell by Liza's unknotted shirt, her mess of a hair, the mismatched buttons of Matt's button down, or her beard burn what they've been up to.

I laugh and shake my head at them, watching from afar as Matt takes her hand, kisses her once, and leads Liza toward the dance floor.

They join the crowd of people on the floor, watching from the sidelines as Barbara and Theo practically steal the show with out-of-this-world dance moves. I mean, the two met in a dance competition, for crying out loud. How could they not?

I laugh at how Theo dips Barbara so low, her long, blonde hair almost sweeps the floor. But then I see the look in their eyes, how they gaze at each other with such depth of emotion and devotion and my heart pangs with sadness.

Yes, I love my friends and I'm so happy that they're happy.

But damn, am I lonely.

I want that.

No. I don't just want that. I want that with one specific person. The one who will never, ever forgive me.

Wanting to eat my feelings, I steal an apple cider donut from my neighbor's plate, untouched from dinner, and scarf it down in three bites. As I wipe the cinnamon sugar off my dress —because *of course* I got it everywhere—I ask myself if things will ever change. Will there ever be a day in which I'll stop feeling this way?

Normally, I can handle these feelings of deep regret, not letting them completely consume me on a day-to-day basis. But today? Seeing Matt and Liza stand up there, under that incredible arch of flowers, and promise themselves to each other for the rest of their lives? That got to me.

How am I supposed to handle my sister's wedding in two months? How am I supposed to handle going back home and run the risk of seeing him and not... completely going to pieces? I've avoided going home for so long...

Lost in a sea of deep regret, I fail to notice John, the owner of the pumpkin farm and party planner failure extraordinaire, walk up to me. "Can I take a seat?" He asks, a little bashfully.

Taken aback a little—mostly because I had spaced out—I stutter, "S-s-sure."

"You have—" He brings his hands to the corners of his mouth.

"Oh, shoot." I bring my napkin to my lips, wiping the cinnamon sugar off my face. "Sorry." And even though I have tanned skin, I can just feel myself flush a deep beet red from having been caught with evidence of my emotional eating all over my face.

"It's not a big deal," he smiles sweetly. "You still look great." John, an average height, but large build man with a face like Ryan Reynolds, blushes like a teenager and looks away, embarrassed.

"Uh, thanks?"

We're quiet for a beat—awkwardly so. After an uncomfortable amount of time that couldn't have been more than two minutes but felt like two hours, I finally break the ice. "Can I help you with something?"

"Oh, ah, no. I mean, I actually—" He clears his throat, his cheeks growing redder by the second, dark eyes looking everywhere but directly at me. This man who looks like a literal movie star with the body of a sexy lumberjack is tongue-tied because of *me*? Doesn't he know that he could have literally anyone in here? I watch as he swallows hard once before continuing. "I was actually wondering whether you'd like to dance? With, ah, with me?"

I feel my jaw drop slightly because, is it the most professional thing in the world for the owner of the venue and alleged organizer of this wedding to be asking a guest to dance when he should be working? I realize he hasn't proved himself to be too knowledgeable about how to run his business based on today's actions, but... Isn't it common sense, though?

I turn my head to look at the dance floor and then back at him. For a minute, I consider dancing with this man. I consider letting myself enjoy a dance—or hell, maybe even a night—with this handsome, perfectly nice guy, feeling his arms wrapped around me all night. I even consider letting him take me on a date if things go okay.

But then I think about John. And about how unfair it would probably be for him. To be out with someone, to think you have potential with this person, and all the while, I'd be wishing I was here with someone else.

I smile ruefully at him, and say, "I'm so sorry. My heels..." I lift the hem of my dress to reveal the gold seventies-style plat-forms I'm wearing. "They're killing me. Thank you, though." A white lie, since, despite their physics-defying height, they're my most comfortable shoes. But I don't want to hurt him. I think it's the perfect blow-off, but then...

"Oh. I'm sorry. Maybe I can just keep you company? Talk? I can hunt down another donut for you, and maybe we can get to know each other a little better?"

The donut is definitely tempting, but the thought of having to sit here and force conversation when I'm feeling like utter *bleep* makes my stomach churn. No offense to John, or anything. So, I suppress a groan and smile once more. "I'm okay, thank you. Don't need much company. You're great I just... Yeah."

He stares blankly at me for a moment before understanding dawns on him and his face flushes red once more. "Oh. I'm *so* sorry. I didn't mean to—"

"No, you're good." I say quickly, not wanting to hurt his feelings. "I'm just... Just not available."

And it's not like it's even a lie. Emotionally, I am completely out of order. Slap a yellow sign on me and tape me off, because this girl is damaged goods.

"Right. Of course." He nods glumly and gets up. "Sorry about that."

"Don't be," I tell him. "Thanks for asking, though."

He smiles reluctantly and walks away, turning only once to look over his shoulder at me.

I wonder how long I'll be able to do this. How long it will take until I'm done feeling this way?

I feel stinging behind my eyes, so I squeeze them shut, ultimately putting a stop to any tear that might want to make its escape. With a sigh, I settle back into my seat once more, rubbing my eyes with my fists, ruining my makeup, I'm sure.

My phone vibrates on the table, so I reach for it to check my notifications. An email from the production company of Barbara's movie has sent me the timeline and itinerary for the five weeks of filming. I review it, and suddenly I feel a little lighter. Maybe this is exactly what I need. Maybe getting out of New York and taking a break from my everyday job and doing something new will help me. Who knows? Maybe I'll meet one of Barbara's super hot costars and fall for one, ultimately leaving behind the idiotic notion that my one true love was someone I met when I was twelve. That I messed things up so badly with him, it's my destiny now to end up alone. Maybe the new guy I meet and I will end up having a whirlwind love story, and live happily ever after.

Or maybe, just maybe, you're a delusional lunatic, Rosie.
Yeah. Maybe.

Feeling a bit suffocated, I decide to take a break from all the music and the crowd. So I take my clutch and wrap and make my way out of the barn. Once I'm finally outside, I lean against the wall a few feet away from the entrance to the reception, out of sight.

With a tightness in my chest, I look up at the stars.

I never realize how much I miss seeing them every night until I'm somewhere where it's an actual possibility. In my hometown in Colorado, looking up at the stars, so clear in the sky, was one of my favorite activities to do with—

Anyway, New York City has so much light pollution from all the buildings, even the thought of ever seeing the stars there is practically laughable.

But it's just as well. If seeing a sky so beautiful like the one tonight can bring back such painful memories, I'm better off that way.

I crane my neck and take in the view, until I catch a shooting star—no, two—*five.*

"Oh my God. It's a *meteor shower,*" I whisper to myself. I gasp and smile up at the sky, taking in this beautiful occasion, admiring this incredible moment and how lucky I am to have caught it. Flashes of bright light shoot through the sky like the fire coursing in my veins. My heart races as I let it wander, let it think about *him.*

The urge to reach out to him, to share this moment with him in even the smallest way, is so intense, suppressing it becomes almost too painful to manage. My hand tightens around my phone, palm growing sweaty.

What would I even text? "*Saw meteor shower, and thought of you?*" "*I miss you and was a total idiot?*"

Would he even reply?

I bring my hand to my chest, rubbing the place where it hurts as the tears start to stream down my cheek.

No.

That's over now. It has to be. I can't go on like this.

And yet...

Sniffling, I pull out my phone and open up my Instagram app. I search for his name, and thank the Lord his profile is still public. He's not the type to be active on there, but he posts a couple of pictures a year. I know his grid by heart, know which picture was uploaded last, like a creepy stalker ex-girlfriend.

Except he was never mine to begin with. Not really.

...Right?

Nine years of this. Nine years of having to live two separate lives after basically spending every waking moment together before that. Nine years and it still feels just as fresh as if it happened yesterday.

I stare up at the meteor shower again and smile through my tears.

He would've loved this.

God, I wish I could call him.

I watch the shower until it's done, pull myself together, and order an Uber to get myself out of there before I get pulled down a dark rabbit hole full of regret.

Asher.

His name is the last thing I think of before I put him back in his box, and mentally lock it up and throw away the key.

Second Chance Snowmance

SEASONS OF LOVE: BOOK 3

PREVIEW!

CAROLINE FRANK

Prologue

ROSIE

18 Years Old - New Year's Eve

Lungs burning as I gasp for air; feet aching in the tightness of my heels, toes cramping, calves hurting; I search for him. A drop of sweat runs down my back as I run through the party, eyes desperately bouncing off every face in the crowd in search of the one person I need most right now.

I check the time on my phone and my stomach turns—11:58 P.M. The countdown will begin soon, and I *still* haven't found him.

Where are you?

Tears puddle in my eyes as desperation floods my system, and I begin to shake. Could be from the blast of chilling air coming from the open doors, or could be the fear of losing the person I love the most for good. The guests move outside onto the patio, ready to ring in the New Year, waiting for the fireworks. They wait for the nighttime ski show that will illuminate the mountain like a blazing trail of fire coming down the slopes as soon as the clock strikes twelve. They gather excitedly, holding onto a balloon with a piece of paper tied to its decorative ribbon. Each guest has written their hopes and wishes for the next year, ready to release them into the sky.

For everyone else, tonight is a night full of hope, of possibilities, of new beginnings and second chances—something I hoped I would get, too. So far, however...

"Ten...nine...eight—"

"No, no, no, no..." I cry under my breath, turning my head in every direction as the crowd cheers. Guests pair up, readying for their midnight kisses, and people tighten their coats around themselves.

"—seven...six...five—"

In a last ditch effort, I decide to run to the bench on the terrace just outside the ballroom. It's where we spent every single New Year together since meeting each other—where I thought I would spend every single one of my New Year's with him.

I race to the bench, trying to see through the crowd of people, hoping to find him before the clock strikes twelve.

A couple moves, and I catch a glimpse of a set of familiar long legs in dark pants and the corner of a red coat sitting on the bench. I smile in relief because *I found him.*

"—four...three—"

With newfound confidence and energy, I push through the guests towards him.

He's been looking for me, too, hoping I'd show up.

It's why he's there; I'm sure of it.

I smile broadly, trying to get to him as quickly as possible. I want us to start the new year together, to fix this, to be together. But as the crowd parts for a brief second, giving me a clear view, my heart rips to shreds.

It's him. He's there. Sitting on our bench on New Year's Eve —just like every other year before. Only this time, his lips are attached to a blonde woman's, one of his hands in her hair, the other grabbing her waist as he brings her closer into him.

"—two...one! *Happy New Year!*"

The crowd erupts into loud cheers as they kiss and release balloons into the air, flooding the sky with silver and gold. The band plays *Auld Lang Syne,* and the guests stop what they're doing to sing along with smiles on their faces, happy that the New Year has begun.

But he doesn't stop. *They* don't stop.

And I keep on staring like a masochist, completely shattered as he uses the hand in her hair to shift her face to his neck. Someone must've punched me in the chest—the heart—because I swear it stops beating.

As if he can hear my sharp inhale over the music and the loud guests, he opens his eyes, immediately meeting mine. They widen for a split second as he holds my gaze, morphing into an unfamiliar hard and cold amber. Gone are the warm and welcoming eyes that always brought me comfort, made me feel safe.

They harden into stone right before he closes them again, and pulls the woman's lips back to his.

Somehow, I manage to make my legs work, and rush out of the party just as the tears streak down my cheeks. Running as fast as I can, I make it to the hotel's front doors, ready to head back home. I push the heavy doors open, but slip on my way out, my vision blurry and head foggy. With a hair-raising *splat,* I fall onto my hands and knees on the ice-covered pavement, pain shooting up and down my arms and legs. Sniffling, I sit up and check myself for injuries, cringing at the sight of blood. Feeling completely deflated, I look up at the sky, trying to see the stars just like we used to do together, lying side by side on his truck bed, on clear nights. But from where I sit, the powder and smoke from the fireworks cloud the night sky, depriving me from the comforting view I so crave.

I can't see the stars anymore and I can't help but wonder whether it's a sign.

I look down at the bloody palms of my hands, my skinned knees, and wince. I finally let the misery overtake me, succumbing to sobs that rip through my chest and make it hard to breathe. Squeezing my eyes shut, I hug my legs to my chest, not caring about the snow or the cold—just needing to take a moment to get myself together.

After what could've been just a few minutes or an hour, I hear a familiar voice behind me—not the one I hoped for, and certainly not one I expected. "Are you okay?" he asks.

My breath hitches in my throat as I raise my head to look at *him*, unchanged. I shake my head slightly, not daring to say a word. He sees the state of my palms and knees and winces.

"You want to come with me? Get you cleaned up?"

His kindness—so unlike him, this man I used to know so well—throws me for a loop. But it's more than welcome after how my heart was broken by the one I truly wanted to spend this night with.

For a moment, I stare deeply into his ice-blue eyes. The last of the New Year's fireworks illuminate his pale face and blonde hair in reds and blues as they burst above us. I consider getting up, and saying no. He's not the one I truly want, after all. I consider going back inside and asking the front desk of the hotel to call me a cab. I consider waiting for someone else to give me a ride.

But I don't want to go home alone tonight, not after what I just witnessed.

So instead, I say, "Yes".

Chapter One

ROSIE

27 Years Old - Present

If you were to tell me right now that Hell isn't a fiery pit of despair, but Denver International Airport during the holiday season, I would believe you. The sheer amount of people running around *Home Alone* 2 style, crashing into me is ridiculous. I get that we're all trying to make it to our final destinations, but damn, can't we all just take a couple of chill pills here?

Working my pastel-pink hair into a loose braid, I wonder idly where all these people came from. I haven't been home in nine years, but I don't remember the airport ever being *this* crowded, even during the holidays. And that's saying something, considering Colorado is a prime ski location.

A man knocks into me from behind with his duffel, and I nearly fall over, catching myself on my pink carry-on. "*Jeez,*" I mutter under my breath. I just want to get out of here, just want the carousel assigned to my flight to start pumping out bags so I can grab my suitcase, get to my bus, and make it home. Not able to help myself, I daydream of the scalding-hot shower I plan on taking as soon as I get home. Of the super-high-waisted, buttery leggings and loose top I plan on slipping into. I yearn for the hours of *Buffy the Vampire Slayer* I'm going to watch in bed with my parents' cat, Manolo, cuddled up next to me.

But mostly I just want that shower. Flying is gross.

Now normally, I'm a carry-on only person through and through. But there was no way I would've been able to achieve it this trip given that I'm coming off of a five-week freelance job on location. *Especially* since I'm a goddamn costume designer with a slight shoe obsession. Not to mention the fact that my little sister is getting married on New Year's Eve, which requires additional outfit changes. Plus, it's Christmas, which means presents, and there was no way I was going to fit every single carefully picked out gift in my small bag along with everything else.

Honestly, it's a miracle I only checked one suitcase, let alone three.

With a loud and shrill noise, the carousel's overlapping metal slats move as bags start tumbling down from a ramp in the ceiling. A large, red duffel falls heavily onto a black suitcase and I wince, realizing now that there is *no way* the glass ornament I got my parents as a Sorry-I've-been-avoiding-coming-home-like-the-plague-all-these-years-but-it's-really-nothing-personal   gift will make it out unharmed.

Fantastic.

Pushing through the crowd to get a little closer to my carousel—one of several in this Arrivals terminal—I look impatiently at the time on my phone. I have about ten minutes to high-tail it outta here if I'm going to make my bus. I shudder to think of what it would mean if I miss it, because *One does not simply hop on the next available one.* The shuttles get booked *weeks* in advance, selling out almost as quickly as they open the reservation slots.

It's really not looking good for me here.

I briefly imagine calling my dad and asking him to make the two-hour drive just to come get me and the drive back, and wince. No, that's out of the question. There's probably no way I'd be able to get a last-minute rental either. A taxi, then? But then, that would probably cost me upwards of two-hundred dollars...

"Hey," I hear a familiar male voice call out behind me. The hairs on the back of my neck rise, every muscle in my body tensing. Suppressing the world's heaviest sigh, I turn to look at the backwards-facing cap-wearing frat bro who talked my ear off the entire two-hour flight here. "Love the braid—it's cute." He reaches out, forcing me to recoil just out of his reach.

Who does this guy think he is? Can he not take a hint? I never once gave him an *ounce* of encouragement the entire flight and now he's back for more rejection?

"I'm Brian, by the way. I just saw you standing here and realized that I never gave you my name and, well, you never gave me yours." His gaze travels up and down my body, taking me in with an appreciative look in his eyes. Though I honestly don't know *what* he thinks he's looking at, because I'm covered in a bulky pink coat and about ten layers of winter clothing underneath.

I press my lips together in a thin line and keep my eyes glued to the carousel.

"Not gonna tell me your name, huh?" He chuckles. "Mystery Girl. I like that." I roll my eyes, but refuse to acknowledge him otherwise. "Anyway, Mystery Girl. I may or may not have read one of your texts over your shoulder while I was sitting next to you on the plane and seen that you're headed to Avon?"

I'm sorry—what?

"I'm headed to Aspen, which is kinda nearby, and I've decided that we're going skiing together. Have a little *après-ski* moment, too." Wiggling his eyebrows, Brian leans in closer, and I pull away from him. *Again.*

"No, thanks. Not much of a skier." And I'm not even lying. I know it might seem like a requirement for someone from the area to ski at an expert level, but I am absolutely lethal on the slopes. And not in a That-girl-is-killing-it-way. More so in an I've-literally-caused-accidents way. Truth is, I moved here from Venezuela when I was 12 and just never got the hang of it.

"That's okay," he smirks. "I was more looking forward to the après-ski than the actual skiing, really."

I shoot him a tight smile. "No, thanks. I'm good."

"C'mon. You're having a drink with me. Non-negotiable."

That's it—I've had enough.

Listen, I'm not one for conflict, but I *really* don't appreciate people pressuring me into doing something I don't want to do— or *shouldn't* do. The last time I almost caved, things did not end well, I can tell you that. So I finally turn to face Brian head-on, ready to tell him off in a *very* direct and impossible to misunderstand manner. "Brian, is it?" He nods, squaring his shoulders proudly. "The thing is—"

I am so ready to put this guy in his place, but suddenly the words get caught in my throat, when something—or rather *someone*—catches my eye over his shoulder.

Asher

My throat tightens and suddenly I'm choking.

Wait, *am* I choking? Is it possible to choke on air? It certainly *feels* that way to me, because I can't get my lungs to work. Maybe I'm suffering from stress-induced paralysis. Or maybe this really *is* hell. Maybe the plane crashed, and I was sent here for my sins, and the universe—or whoever the hell (haha, get it?) manages this place—just *knew* to trap me in this over-crowded airport with a man who refuses to leave me alone, only to be haunted by the worst mistake of my entire, short, twenty-seven years of life.

This is definitely hell. I totally just died.

It's such a tragedy, really. I was *so* young. I still had so much to live for. I mean, I was still waiting to hear back about that promotion! Being the Head Costume designer for *Celebrity Dance Battle* would have been incredible. Plus, I had tickets for my friend Barbara's musical in January. I'd even been toying with the idea of adopting a cat! Regret floods my system, filling my head with a sudden influx of missed opportunities and untaken vacations.

But then... Then I pull my head out of my ass and realize that maybe I am being just *a little bit* dramatic, and that there is a 99.9999999% chance that I really am still alive and standing here like an idiot, completely slack-jawed, staring at a man I haven't seen in almost nine years to the date.

I watch him run his fingers through his dark hair as he looks back to his carousel and remember exactly what it felt like when *I* did it.

A sudden sharp intake of breath, and my chest expands, filling with air.

Yes. Oxygen. Good. I need some of that.

My eyes are laser-focused on every movement he makes, every expression on his face, taking in just how much he's changed physically, but also remained the same.

God, he looks good. He still looks young, of course, but more of a man now. Broader shoulders, slightly shorter hair, and did he get taller? Or maybe I just got shorter.

I certainly feel small right now...

I watch him as he pulls a forest green suitcase from the carousel slats with ease, making it look as light as a feather. With a heartbreaking smile, he hands it to an older lady. My heart squeezes in my chest at the gesture, because he's still the type of guy that helps strangers out without even thinking twice about it. So much has changed since we last saw each other, but it's nice to know that at least that hasn't.

I know I was in the middle of doing something, but I can't for the life of me remember what that was. My eyes glued to him, I watch each of his fluid movements like a hawk. The way he runs the back of his hand over his travel stubble, how he rubs his eyes in a sign of tiredness under his round, tortoise glasses (a nice upgrade from the black, hipster ones he used to wear in high school), and how he readjusts the strap of his backpack over his shoulder.

All of a sudden, it hits me: I look like absolute crap. "Oh my God," I mutter under my breath.

"What? What's wrong?" a voice I recognize asks, buzzing like a mosquito in my ear: annoying and distracting.

I ignore it and take stock of myself; of my disheveled hair, gross from travel; of the fact that I feel puffy and bulky (and probably look that way, too).

He *cannot* see me like this. The first time I see Asher Wolff after nine years *cannot* be like this.

I've thought of this moment about a million times. About what I would say, how I would act. How I would casually greet him, cool as a cucumber; as if I had built a bridge over him and everything that had happened between us, and gotten over it. I even planned out what I would wear, of course: that black wrap dress that looks like nothing on a hanger, but only does amazing things to my body when I wear it—the one currently neatly folded in my suitcase. The color is really off-brand for me, but the whole outfit makes my legs look longer, my waist snatched, my butt appear smaller. It has *just* the right amount of cleavage that my boobs look fantastic, but still leaves something for the imagination. All this time I had imagined my hair would be in soft waves down my back, my toasted skin would be glowy, and I'd be wearing that one shade of red lipstick he once drunkenly admitted to liking so much.

For Christ's sake, I would have at least worn Spanx!

Asher, on the other hand, looks amazing. The combination of the tweed blazer peaking just under his coat and those glasses make him look like an academic snack I'd love to spread on a cracker, thank you very much. A nerdy, sexy professor I wouldn't mind spending the afternoon in detention with, if you know what I mean.

As I continue to watch him, I wonder what he's been up to these past few years. Normally, I try not to let my thoughts stray there. But when your families are so close, it's hard to isolate yourself completely from any information regarding the man you used to love.

Or currently love. It's hard to tell sometimes.

Last I heard, he was in a Ph.D. program, but I'm not sure which or where. Did he decide to pursue his doctorate in Astrophysics like he planned on while we were still friends? Or did he decide to focus on a different topic?

After a few seconds' consideration, I decide there's no way he'd ever give up that dream. He was way too passionate about the topic not to pursue it. Even though years have passed since seeing him, I know who Asher is to his core. I'd bet every shoe in my closet he never gave up on his dream.

Despite vowing to limit my knowledge of Asher's life, I had to prepare myself mentally to see him again. According to my mother, Asher wasn't supposed to make it to my sister's wedding *or* the holidays this year—he was too busy.

Clearly, I had been ill-informed.

As I watch him, I wonder what he's doing in Colorado. I watch as he effortlessly pulls another bag from the carousel—this time, a familiar, worn black duffel—and straps it over one shoulder. With a last wave to the woman he helped, Asher makes his way toward the car rental desks... The ones that are coincidentally right next to my carousel.

This is it. There's no avoiding it.

I groan in frustration, horror. I mean, I had a plan. One that did not involve me looking like *this*. I *definitely* wouldn't be wearing a million layers of clothing, have bags under my eyes, and have gross hair that looks like—

Wait... Wait one second. My hair!

He's never seen me with pink hair before! He's only ever seen me in its natural jet-black color.

Yes, perfect. He'll never notice me like this. All I have to do is—

Fuck.

I swear it happens in slow motion—or at least it feels that way. But, as if sensing my eyes on him, Asher slowly turns his head in my direction, his gaze locking on mine. Eyes widening, he stops mid-step. For a second, an expression I can't quite make out flashes over his beautiful, amber eyes. He swallows once, adjusts his glasses on his face, and slowly brings his left hand up to give me a slow wave with one of those lopsided smiles of his I remember so well.

My stomach drops, and I stop breathing again. Feeling like I've been caught with my hand in the cookie jar, I lift my hand and wave back. I do my best to smile in return, but it's like I've forgotten which muscles I need to do so. I'm pretty sure the best I can manage is a mangled grimace of sorts, because his grin wavers slightly.

With a deep breath, he changes course and makes his way to

me, each of his steps matching the steady drumming in my chest...

Step. Ta-dum. Step. Ta-dum. Step. Ta-dum.

When his eyes fall to the man beside me, his stride falters—and so does my heart. Mortified, I do my best to call upon the uncanny talent we used to have to read each other's thoughts. *No way. I'm not with him,* I try to tell him. But it seems like our powers of telepathy have disappeared and faded into nothingness, along with our friendship.

Finally—after what feels like another decade—Asher stops a few feet from me.

With those amber eyes never leaving mine, he breathes, *"Rosie."*

Chapter Two

ROSIE

The sound of my name on his lips is like a starter pistol to my heart. It jumps and races into a full-on spree. So much so, that I unconsciously bring my hand to my chest in a half-assed attempt to slow it down, tell it to chill, begging it to stop aching.

Come on, girl. Don't do this to me.

"Rosie." He says it again, as if getting used to uttering my name aloud after all these years. Without hesitation, Asher drops his duffel and opens his arms broadly in invitation, and suddenly find that I can't help myself. I go to him.

Sure, I've spent the past nine years literally doing everything possible to avoid ever seeing him again. But I can't help taking the opportunity to feel his arms around me one more time. Like gravity, his pull is absolute and undeniable.

"It's so good to see you." He murmurs into my hair, arms tightening around my waist. But I can barely process it because the entire time I should be enjoying this moment, I ask myself, "Is *it good to see me? Because I would've bet my life that you hated me*". I'm sure that I'm giving myself too much credit, though, because of course he's over it—it's been nine years.

He drops his arms and takes a single step back before saying,

"It's been too long". His voice is deeper than I remembered, but still smooth and delicious. It reaches every corner of my soul, soothing some of the pain I'd gotten used to after all this time.

Asher's enthusiasm is contagious—suddenly, I'm not *completely* mortified to have run into him. And then that sparkly feeling I always used to feel around him makes a surprising reappearance after lying dormant for so long. I feel it shine in my chest, like bright lights fighting to get out, to burst through.

Finally, a huge smile spreads on my face because, *oh my God*, Asher is here. He's *here*, standing right in front of me and it's been so long since I've seen him and sure, we lost touch because of the whole "incident" but whatever, who cares because *he's here*.

"Asher." His name feels foreign on my lips; it almost burns my tongue.

"You changed your hair!" He laughs, reaching out to touch my braid. He stops himself right before, though, dropping his hand, frowning at it as he clenches it into a fist.

I would have let you touch it. I would have let you undo my braid, run your fingers through it.

He collects himself and grins down at me again, amber eyes bright with excitement. He's so beautiful, I stare up at him, completely awestruck. I have to crane my neck because, at six-four, Asher is a full foot taller than me, making me feel smaller than I usually already do. As my eyes travel over his handsome, angular face, I realize that my memory didn't do him justice. His expectant smile dazzles me, and I can barely open my damn mouth to say a single word.

"Yeah." She speaks! Now I just need to add a few more words, weave them into a logical sentence, and... "Quite a long time ago, actually." Wow. *Two* whole sentences. Yay me!

Asher bends to pick up his duffel, swinging its strap over his shoulder again. "I shouldn't be surprised. You always wanted to color it, and your obsession with pink always ran *deep*," he chuckles, and the reminder that we once knew each other so well stings a little. "It's the reason I started calling you Rosie, after all."

I squint my eyes and tilt my head to the side, bringing my hand to my chin in an exaggerated, mock-thinking expression. "Was it? Or was it because you couldn't pronounce my name correctly as kids and thought it would also serve as a great *gringo* nickname for Rosario?"

He laughs softly, his eyes bright. "Hey, necessity is the mother of invention. I didn't know how to speak Spanish well back then, and my pronunciation sucked. And am I to assume that now, suddenly, I'm a *gringo*? Didn't you once tell me I was and forever will be an honorary Venezuelan? Don't I get any points for years of you imposing your *delicious* foods, customs, music, and slang?"

It gets you all the points. Whatever you want.

"Imposing," I scoff. "But, I guess so. I guess you deserve *some* credit," I say as we grin stupidly at each other.

"Plus, the nickname stuck, didn't it?" He's right. Everyone calls me Rosie now—except for Dad.

A throat clears behind me, causing me to jolt. "Hey, man." Brian outstretches his hand towards Asher, as he edges himself between us. I feel my cheeks flush crimson red in embarrassment—partly because I *completely* forgot about the other human standing right beside me, and partly because I feel oddly compelled to clarify that I am very single.

Weird.

"The name's Brian. How's it going?" But it's not really a question, is it?

Asher looks down at my kind-of-stalker's hand with a

confounded look on his face. Addressing me with an amused, but tight smile, he asks, "Boyfriend?"

I nearly choke on air again.

My mouth opens to answer him with a big, fat *hell, no*, but am quickly cut off by Brian himself. "Nah, man. We just met. But we *are* going on a date. Right?" He winks at me and then looks back at Asher, who catches me rolling my eyes at Brian. He gives up on shaking Asher's hand and drops his, shoving it inside his coat pocket.

"Um." My eyes flash to Asher's, his smile wavering as he watches me. "I'm flattered, Brian. But I'm here with my family, so that's going to be a hard pass for me."

Frowning, Brian slips his hand into his other pocket, pulls out a white card, and hands it to me with a wry smile. "Here. Call me *when* you change your mind." Brian winks once at me and walks away—but not before shooting a glaring look at Asher, who merely snorts in his direction.

More out of habit than anything else, I slip Brian's business card into my purse, planning on throwing it out as soon as I can. Asher looks down at me with an expression of curiosity in his eyes, but says nothing. Meanwhile, I take in his perfect, dark curly hair, his slightly crooked nose, with that slight bump on the bridge of it from when he broke it in high school. I take in his large hands, the ones who knew exactly what to do with me, even when they didn't.

An awkward pause hangs heavy between us before Asher clears his throat and says, "So, are you taking the bus home or...?"

I stare up at him, completely bewildered. "Huh? The—? *Oh, no!*" I pull my phone out and check the time. "I missed my bus!" I groan, putting my face in my hands. "My bags, too!" I turn back to my carousel and, lo-and-behold, my pink suitcase is the last one on the slats, spinning around, looking lonely and abandoned.

"Wait here." Because even though I've spent all these years avoiding Asher, it only took one second to never want to say goodbye ever again. I jog the few feet back to my flight's carousel, dragging my carry-on behind me. I wait for my bag to make the trip around one last time but, just as I'm about to reach for it, a muscular arm gets ahead of me and pulls it out with ease.

"Damn, Rosie. This weighs a ton," Asher says, his voice laced with amusement as he sets the bag beside me. "You got a body in here or something?"

"Two, actually. My latest victims." His laughter floods my chest with warmth, and suddenly I feel like crying. This is why I didn't want to come back here. *This* is why. We've spent less than an hour together, and I can already tell it's going to be hell readjusting to life without him again.

Another awkward silence. Not a single word passes between us, but a lot is said, the spark reviving itself from the ashes of two people who burned each other down.

Or maybe it was just me. Maybe I was the only one doing the burning.

Something suddenly grips my heart and the words *"Forgive me"* get caught in my throat, begging to be spoken aloud. Nothing comes out, though. I'm a coward. I'm not proud of it, but them's the facts.

There are... so many things I want—*need*—to say. Overwhelmed with emotion, not knowing what will come out first, I open my mouth to say something, but he cuts me off: "So...I'm guessing you need a ride?" With a smirk, he adds, "It's not like you're *too* far out of my way."

Did I mention we were childhood neighbors?

Chapter Three

ASHER

Rosie Castillo

It might not be the most macho thing in the world to admit, but I'm not gonna deny that seeing her standing there by baggage claim didn't momentarily make my heart stop and then restart with so much adrenaline I legitimately felt like I was having a goddamn heart attack.

But it's fine. I'm cool. I'm not freaking out—you're freaking out.

"You really didn't have to do this, you know. I could've waited for another bus." She settles more comfortably in the seat of my rental—a pretty spacious Honda CRV—and I can tell that the travel exhaustion is finally catching up with her. "Or gotten a cab. It's really not a big deal."

Her mouth says one thing, but her eyes tell a different tale. I scoff, shooting her a disbelieving glance—because is she insane? "Like I was gonna let you pay two-hundred bucks for a cab. Are you kidding? And why would you make yourself wait hours for the next available shuttle in that hellhole of an airport when I could just give you a free ride?"

"*Hellhole*, indeed." She suppresses a smile. "At least let me pay for half of the rental fee."

"Not a chance. Besides, you know how much I *love* road trips with you. They're never uneventful. Which reminds me... Did you remember to use the restroom before we left?" I try to control my laughter, but damn, I can't help it as it bursts through.

Rosie sucks in a sharp breath and narrows her eyes at me. "I *cannot* believe you'd bring our trip to CU - Boulder up," she hisses, cheeks flushing a deep red. "I thought we agreed never to talk about it again."

"It's kind of hard to forget," I chuckle, remembering the road trip fondly. It was hours of being stuck in the car, having her all to myself, as she sang—*very* poorly—at the top of her lungs. *Of course* I let her take over the radio, so it was hours of torturous Gaga and Adele, pop music I couldn't stand, but knew she loved.

But fuck me if it wasn't the best trip of my life.

The part where she peed her pants was an unfortunate, yet hilarious, cherry on top of it all. However, it made her look a little more human to me; a little less of an unattainable fantasy. But she doesn't know that. All I tell her is, "It was definitely more memorable of an experience than the prospective students tour we went on."

Embarrassment disguised as rage flashes across her face and spills out through her words. "It wasn't my fault! I can't believe I'm having to defend myself again, ten years later. We were stuck on that stupid highway for *five* hours in bumper-to-bumper traffic with no rest stop in sight. It's not like I *wanted* to pee my pants." Rosie crosses her arms in front of her chest and bitterly looks out the window.

I burst out laughing again. "God, that was hilarious. Thank

god Mom's car seats were pleather and not fabric. Easy clean-up."

She groans, putting her face in her hands. "I'm not enjoying this particular walk down memory lane, Asher. But if you're going to insist on it, pick a better moment in our history to revisit. *Please.*" Sharp words slice through me, leaving a trail of paralyzing and painful venom.

I gasp quietly, shocked by her reaction. I was just trying to bring back what I *thought* were good memories from our past in order to avoid the unpleasant ones. Excuse me for misreading things. *Again.*

My jaw tightens, trying not to go there.

Ten years ago, she probably would've groaned, shoved my shoulder, and told me to leave her the hell alone or risk exposing one of *my* dirty secrets. But so much has changed... What did I expect? For things to go back to normal? What even *is* normal now anyway?

"I—I'm sorry. I didn't mean to bring up...*bad* memories between us. But I guess there are always two sides to every story, right? Because I just remember having so much fun. Some of my favorite memories come from that two-week road trip we took to visit schools." The entire time, I keep my eyes on the road. It's a clear, sunny day, but you'd think we were in the middle of a snowstorm from how focused I am on my driving. "I didn't mean to upset you. I guess I remember things a little differently than you do." A pause. "As usual."

Okay, that was a low blow. But I tell myself it's the one and only comment I'll make about everything that happened.

"It's fine," she mumbles. "I—I overreacted. Just tired from travel and work, and I'm a bit anxious to see my family again."

I latch immediately onto the topic of her family, wanting desperately to steer the conversation away from us. Correction: from me and Rosie.

Silly Asher. There's no "us" for you.

"C'mon, they're not so bad." The corners of my mouth quirk up a little in a half-assed attempt at a smile, and the tension in the car seems to lift ever-so-slightly.

"You say that because you aren't related to them. Plus, I know for a fact my parents love you more than they love me—you can do no wrong in their eyes. I, on the other hand, am their biggest disappointment."

I *tsk* and shake my head.

"Seriously. I think Mom is proud of me, but Dad..." she sighs. "Dad is... Well, you know. I'm sure they would both rather I had taken a different path in life. Though I don't think they agree on which one."

I frown, wanting to ask her if things have gotten worse, but stop myself just in time. Distance. I need to keep some sort of distance here, or I won't survive the rest of the holidays.

"Just the thought of having to spend the next ten days with them, having to listen to them criticize my work, my life, and even the way I look exhausts me."

"What's wrong with the way you look?" I ask, a sense of protectiveness flaring.

"The pink hair?" Rosie points to her head, with a *Duh* expression on her face.

"Ah." I nod before thoughtlessly adding, "Well, for what it's worth, I like the way you look."

Fuck.

I shouldn't have said that, right? That was weird. Was it weird? Okay, it was definitely weird.

Fantastic.

Though it sure as hell wasn't a lie; Rosie has *always* been beautiful. And now, nine years later, she's all curves and big, dark brown eyes—fucking gorgeous. And though her pink hair isn't natural, she's never looked more comfortable in her own skin than she does now. Rosie Castillo is so beautiful, I could barely breathe when I saw her standing there in the airport. Even now, it takes everything to keep my cool knowing that she's sitting next to me. My hands are aching to touch her, just to make sure she isn't some sort of hallucination.

My chest aches as I try to steer my mind away from how my body so easily reacts to hers.

"I just meant, the pink hair suits you," I push out.

Nice save, idiot.

"Thanks," she whispers.

I nod once, clearing my throat. My eyes have never been more focused on the road ahead of me, and still I see how my one little comment makes her toasted skin flush.

"Anyway. I'm just trying to prepare myself. Mom is gonna do everything in her power to get me to move back home—she'll start by saying things like '*Ay*, Rosie. Aren't the mountains *increíbles?* You definitely don't get this view in New York,'" she says, mimicking her mother's Spanish accent. "Dad is going to lecture me about my career choice and how I made a colossal mistake going into fashion and costume design. He thinks I can still switch into something '*serious*'"—she air-quotes—"like finance." I try to control my smile as I realize she's about to go on one of her impassioned rants I used to love so much, with that sexy barely-noticeable accent. Glad some things never change.

"But Diana will *insist* I find a man and settle down and have a family. She thinks she's being a protective older sister telling me to give up on any professional dreams I may have just like she did, but it's like she doesn't know me at all. I'd give up my kidney before giving up my career for some guy."

I shift uncomfortably in my seat, my fists tightening around the steering wheel at her words. I shouldn't be surprised by them, though; I've learned from harsh experience she means what she says.

"We don't all have to have the same dreams or definitions for success, you know? I'm up for a promotion at *Celebrity Dance Battle*; I'm growing in the industry. Why can't they see that?"

She stops, exhales. "Sorry. It's a touchy subject."

"I'll say," I laugh. The topic of Rosie's family not really approving of her life choices has *always* been a touchy subject.

"Plus, everyone is going to be extra stressed because of Andrea's wedding. I predict this to be far from a relaxing holiday vacation."

"Oh, I could totally see that," I chuckle.

"I assume you're coming, then?"

I nod and she hums thoughtfully before turning her head to look out the window.

"Why?"

She shrugs. "Oh, nothing. It's just, mom had said you weren't going to make it, which is why I was a little surprised to see you at the airport."

I frown, my eyes on the road. "Really? That's weird. I RSVP'd months ago." And I've been anxious about seeing her ever since. I knew she hadn't been home in years, but I was positive she wouldn't miss her sister's wedding.

Still, I never expected to run into her *the second* I got to Colorado.

Out of the corner of my eye, I watch as Rosie fidgets with her fingers and mutters something unintelligible in Spanish under her breath.

"Is—Is that a problem?" I ask hesitantly.

"What? No. And what about your sister? Is she coming for the holidays?"

"Jessica's husband got transferred to Ramstein Air Base in Germany last year. They're spending the holidays eating *stollen torte* and whatever the hell else German people do on Christmas. But she'll be back home in time for the wedding."

"Awesome," she smiles brightly. "I haven't seen Jess in ages."

I press my lips together, my jaw tightening.

Don't be a dick. Don't be a dick. Don't be a dick.

I nod and clear my throat. "Yeah, well. I noticed you haven't been home in a while. I mean, I haven't seen you around here in years. Not since—" I cut myself off. "Well. You know. Not since that New Year's, right?"

I regret the words as soon as they leave my mouth; cursing myself for acknowledging that night. I should've played innocent.

"Um..." Rosie fidgets in her seat. "I—I've been busy."

"Busy." An ice-cold word so sharp it cuts like glass.

"Yes. Busy. You know. Life. Work. Et cetera."

Et cetera.

The urge to snort is strong, but I manage to restrain myself. With a cold, dark voice that I can't help, I parrot, "Et cetera."

"Yes."

After a few minutes of silence, she speaks again: "I'm gonna call my mom, if that's okay with you." She rummages for her phone in her purse.

"Sure."

"*Aló?*" The volume is up high enough on Rosie's phone that I hear Julieta's voice, bright and enthusiastic. In the background on the other end of the line, I hear voices laughing and chatting away loudly in Spanglish.

"*Hola, Mami.* I'm on my way home from the airport. Should be there in an hour and a half or so."

"Great! So you made the bus, then? Your father was scared you wouldn't make it, but I told him it would be fine."

"Oh, um, actually..." Her eyes flash to me. "No, I didn't

make it in time for the shuttle bus. But it's fine, because I... I ran into Asher at the airport. He's giving me a ride home."

There's silence on the other end of the line, the sound of a hand covering the receiver, and a muffled whisper.

"*Ma?*" she asks over the snickers.

"*Sí, amor.* We're—" A truck blares its horn beside us, so I miss what Julieta says. "—with his mom at the house, so you should tell Asher to come and say hi when he drops you off before he heads home. It's been so long since I've seen him."

It doesn't surprise me to hear that my mom is at the Castillos', since our mothers are very close. When their family moved to the United States, my mom befriended Rosie's, and helped her with the acclimatization process. Julieta saw a single mother struggling to balance work and her two kids, and took all three of them in.

The Castillos were used to having a big family around them, which they had lost with their move. As I understood it, we not only filled that void they seemed to miss, but overflowed it.

Meanwhile, we were in search of love and support after having experienced so much loss in such a short amount of time. First, with my father leaving us, and six months later, with the sudden passing of my grandfather.

Very quickly, our families integrated, sharing holidays and vacations, school pickups—you name it.

Rosie's and my friendship was inevitable.

Loving her was fate.

"Yeah, I'll tell him. We should be home soon." Julieta inhales sharply, and Rosie rolls her eyes—at what, I don't know. She hangs up with a sigh, shoving her phone into her bag.

"Your mom is at my parents'. She said to stop by before you go to yours." I nod once. She pauses. "They're making *hallacas.*"

I do my best to control my facial features from revealing the wave of emotions crashing over me. Is this a joke? Is today just a whole fucking cosmic joke? Is this the universe trying to be ironic or something? Because not only did we just happen to run into each other *at the airport*, but now, the first time I see her in nine years will be on the same day they're making *hallacas*? The first time we see each other happens to fall on the same day—

Is this us coming full circle? The sign of the beginning of the end of my story with Rosie?

Seriously, what did I ever do to the universe to deserve this shit? Is it because it's my life's calling to uncover its secrets? It's like it's laughing at me, wanting to twist the knife inside of me, when I just want to get out of this holiday alive.

Screw you, universe.

I nod once, terrified she'll see the emotions coursing through me, terrified to see hers. Or worse—and the more likely of options—the complete lack of connection or acknowledgment in them.

Does she even remember? Does she even remember what it means to us?

From the corner of my eye, I watch as she rubs her chest over her sternum, tired. Her brows pull together as she exhales deeply. With a frown, my anger melts as concern for her overtakes it. "You can sleep, if you want. I mean, we don't have to talk the entire way there."

I turn to look at her and watch her push back slightly into the seat, her eyes widening in surprise before the hurt takes over. Did she think—? Oh, shit.

"Yeah, you're right. We don't have to talk—it's best if we don't." She blinks back tears and keeps her eyes straight on the road.

Horrified with myself, I quickly try to fix the misunderstanding: "I—I didn't mean it like that." My words come out hurried; I can't say them fast enough. "Rosie, I only meant because you mentioned you were tired and—"

"No, no. I understand. Don't worry," her voice breaks on the last word and I hate myself for it. She unwraps her scarf from around her neck, bundling it up into a ball into a makeshift pillow against the passenger window. "I'm just going to nap. You're right—I need the energy if I'm going to deal with a full house as soon as I get home."

"Rosie—" But she holds a hand up to stop me before closing her eyes and laying her head on the bunched up scarf, shutting me out. I watch her squeeze her eyes shut, lips pressed together.

My gaze turns back to the road with a loud exhale.

What a fucking nightmare. I didn't want this. I didn't want it to be like this. Whenever I thought of seeing Rosie again after so long, I promised myself I wouldn't let her see how affected I was by her presence. I promised myself I would be as friendly and open as possible—that I wouldn't let our past define the present. We wouldn't be friends anymore, but I didn't want there to be any anger or resentment between us.

I thought it had gone well, for the most part. But there's no denying that the damage done will be a little harder to leave in the past than I expected.

But don't I get props for being able to drive and talk all while trapped in this fucking car with her? With her scent and her voice and her face and just everything about her reopening wounds I worked hard to close?

God, this is a nightmare.

My heart races as memories of happier times flash before my eyes. Of Christmases past, of the first one we spent together, the instant we became friends. Memories of laughter, and being understood, and *hallacas*...

Chapter Four

ROSIE

12 Years Old

Papi *says that the best way to get used to this is to make the effort to think in English. He also said that he and* Mami *aren't going to speak to us in Spanish anymore, which I don't like.*

Before coming here, I already spoke English well. I think. But Papi *still made sure we took intensive English lessons after school every day before our move. Just like he did when he was our age.*

He later went on to study hospitality in this country when he was a college student before moving back home. Or I guess this is home now, and Venezuela... isn't. Not anymore.

I try to shake away the sadness, the fear of being in a new place, so different from what I'm used to, praying my language skills get better soon.

Mami *says I need to get better because I start school after the new year, so I'm not even allowed to speak Spanish with my sisters. This morning, I asked Diana for her to pass me the* mantequilla *for my* arepa, *and she yelled at me.*

"We need to do our best to do good—well—here, Rosario. This

new job is important for Papi and our family. This is our new life," Diana *had said.*

New life.

Diana is really good at speaking the language—almost as good as Papi. I think it's because she watched a lot of TV in English back home.

Mami *says Andrea will learn fast because she's only eight and so young, and that it might be a little harder for me. But I'm twelve and that's young, right?*

"Rosario! Come down to do the hallacas!" Mami *calls.* "And we have company. You have to meet, eh..." *she struggles to find the right words.* Mami's English *is not so good either.* "The..." *I hear her blow a frustrated puff of air as I walk down the stairs towards the kitchen.* "The neigh—neighbor? Jaime and her son."

I turn into the kitchen and see a woman and a boy sitting at the table. The mother smiles at me behind her cup of coffee, while the boy beside her lays his chin on his folded hands, which rest on the table. When his eyes, hidden behind thick glasses, meet mine, I see his cheeks pink, and he sits up in his chair.

"Asher, say hi to Mrs. Castillo's daughter."

"Rosario," *my mother clarifies.*

The boy fixes his glasses before asking, "Did you know that the grey wolf travels in packs of seven or eight? And even though they have complex communication skills, they don't really howl at the moon like in the movies?"

I stare at the boy and take a seat across from him. "No. I did not know that."

His mother laughs nervously, her eyes moving between the two of us. "Asher likes fun facts like that." *She makes a face and he looks up at her with a hurt look in his eyes.*

"It's supposed to serve as a conversation starter," *he mutters, looking down at his hands with a scowl.*

His mother leans in closer to mine and whispers, "I'm sorry.

112

Asher doesn't have many friends, so he's not used to kids his own age."

"I like wolves," I say, speaking up. It's not like I love them, but I don't mind the piece of information. It's...interesting.

The boy—Asher—looks up and meets my eyes, a broad smile appearing on his face.

There's a moment of silence as we stare at each other. Eventually, Mami breaks the silence: "Would you like to stay over for dinner? We're making hallacas."

Jaime tilts her head in confusion. "What are those?"

"They're like...Mexican tamales? But they're Venezuelan and I think they taste better. They have the stuffing of different meats, wrapped in plátano leaves." Mami winces, struggling to find the right words. "We eat them at Christmas on the twenty-fourth. For us, it's a tradition to have all the women in the family gather to cook them as a group around Christmas." Mami frowns, her eyes watering.

"This year, I don't have my sisters or mother here—just my girls. But would you like to join? You can take some home with you if you like them. Diego—my husband—is shopping with my other daughters for the rest of the ingredients, but they will be back soon. Maybe you can ask your daughter?" It's the most I've heard Mami speak in English at one time, and I'm so proud—I know it took a lot of effort.

Mami looks hopeful, the idea of a new friend bringing some much-needed light back into her eyes. Smiling, Asher's mom puts her coffee cup back down on the table. "Sure. Jessica, my daughter, is at a friend's house. But I'd love to help—though I'm not much of a cook, if I'm being honest."

The boy chuckles a bit and shoots me a smirk.

"Will you stay, too?" I ask him.

Asher smiles broadly at me and says—

Chapter Five

ROSIE

"Rosie." I hear a male voice somewhere in the distance. "Rosie, wake up."

Asher.

"Mmmm." I groan, wanting to go back to the beginning.

"Rosie." A warm hand shakes me gently by the shoulder. "Wake up—we're here."

Sitting up with a jolt, my eyes fly open and our gazes immediately lock. Asher slowly smiles at me as I process my surroundings, trying to remember where I am. "Oh." Just one look out the window tells me that we're parked right in front of my parents' house. "We're home," I breathe.

"You good?" He asks, popping the trunk open. I nod, rubbing the newly-formed knot in my neck as he exits the car with the surprising agility of a jungle cat. Seriously, how can a man so tall be so graceful?

Stiff with sleep, I struggle to pull myself out of the car and help him with our bags. "Don't worry about my stuff. I've got it."

"No, it's fine. I don't mind." He smiles down at me, and for a moment, I feel that light building in my chest again.

"*Finalmente!* My daughter is home!" My mother comes

barreling out the front door and down the porch step, interrupting the very brief moment Asher and I were sharing. She engulfs us in her arms, squeezing us tightly together.

I wrap my free arm around her—the one that isn't pressed up against Asher's side—and roll my eyes. "*Mami*, we just saw each other in Florida a couple of months ago. Chill."

"*Sí*, but not like this. It's not the same as having you here for the holidays, *amor*." She pushes back and holds both my arms between her hands in an iron grip. "*Dios mío*, look at all this pink hair," she says, tugging at it. "When are you going to dye it dark again?"

I roll my eyes at her and push her hand away, bracing myself for more. "It's been too long since you've been here, Rosie. And that's not okay. *Mira!* Look how beautiful this place is! And how fresh the air is here. You definitely won't get a view like this anywhere else." I suppress a snort, and look over at Asher, who's smirking.

Told you so.

Turning my attention back to my mother, I say, "I'm here now. Isn't that what counts?"

My mother rolls my eyes and pulls me back into her arms—just me this time. After a few seconds, she lets me go and hugs Asher. My heart does that achy thing it's been doing as I see him happily wrap his arms around her. I rub my chest where it hurts.

"*Ashercito*,"—the *sh* in his name sounding more like a *ch*—"How are you? I haven't seen you since this summer." *This summer?* "I've missed you."

Jealousy shoots through me like adrenaline. My mother gets to so openly express her genuine emotions with him freely. Meanwhile, I need to repress the sudden onslaught of emotions that have overtaken me since seeing him just a few hours ago.

He chuckles lightly. "It's good to see you, too." He kisses the top of her head and releases her. "My mother? Why didn't she come running out to meet me, huh?" He smiles teasingly.

"She went back to your house, *amor*. She had to speak with one of the buyers." Asher nods pensively.

"Buyers?" I stop in my tracks and look over at Asher, who stares back at me with a sympathetic look in his eyes.

"Yeah, ah. Mom's—" He clears his throat. "Mom's selling the store."

A sharp inhale of freezing cold air feels like icicles stabbing my lungs. "She's selling *Seymour's*?"

"Actually, it's already sold. But we have until December thirty-first to clean it up and hand it over."

A wave of disbelief crashes over me, because—No.

"B-B-But—"

No. It's where we grew up; where Asher and I worked for three summers. It's where I had my first kiss, right there in the dark stock room with the one flickering lightbulb.

Asher's pained eyes scan my face because I know he's also reliving an entire adolescence in one place—one we shared. "A new developer wants to make a big condo building there. They made Mom an offer she couldn't refuse."

For the second time today, my jaw drops in surprise. "But Asher... That's—That's your grandfather's shop." As if he didn't already know. My voice cracks on the last word because that place was like our sanctuary—our treehouse, of sorts. I know I have no actual claim to it, but I feel hurt no one felt the need to mention this to me.

Asher can see my pain, though, because he shares it. "I know," he whispers.

Mom pushes past me. "Let's not talk about this now." She turns and waves for us to follow, while he straps his suitcase over one shoulder, lugging mine behind him. "Come inside for a minute to say hi to the girls. We've been cooking all day. Then I'll let you go back to your mother."

Asher chuckles softly, but otherwise agrees.

The state of disarray in my mother's kitchen doesn't really surprise me, nor does the loud, collective greeting from the women sitting around the kitchen table. Even if it's been a while, I know for a fact that *hallacas*-making day is all about drinking wine, bonding, and eating—*a lot*.

What does throw me is the unexpected feeling of homesickness brought upon by seeing these familiar faces in my childhood kitchen, all while partaking in a deeply significant tradition for our family. We've done it several times over the years, but I obviously haven't been able to be part of one in a while, leaving me feeling left out.

My little sister is the first one to greet me, abandoning her plantain leaf *hallaca*-wrapping duties, and rising from her seat to pull me quickly into her arms. "Rosie! Oh my god, you're here!"

I wrap my arms around my favorite sister, and breathe her in, letting the happiness of this sweet reunion spread over me like a relieving balm of some kind. It's been a tense couple of hours, and it's nice to have an ally.

Where I'm short and curvy, Andrea is a half foot taller and model-thin. Basically a Latin goddess, with her malachite green eyes and black-as-night long, wavy hair, my little sister has always been considered "the pretty one" in the family. But as if it weren't enough to make her incredibly beautiful, God or the universe or biology or whatever, made her one of the best people in existence, as well. Fiercely loyal, incredibly kind, and absolutely brilliant, Andrea is the whole package, making her fiancé the luckiest man in the world. "I've missed you so much!"

I hug her tightly, inhaling her sweet coconut scent, squeezing my eyes shut to avoid a tear creeping out.

I've missed her, too.

Growing up, Andrea and I never really bonded or anything. When you're a kid and a teenager, a four-year age gap is pretty big. But a few years ago, just before lockdown began, Andrea had come to New York City for a job interview. What was supposed to be her crashing on my couch for a couple of days became months of being locked in my apartment together. We got to know each other as adults, making the best out of a terrible situation.

For the first time in years, I wasn't running away from closeness to people from my past. Unfortunately, Andrea didn't end up getting the job she wanted, leaving her to take the only one she was offered: a wealth-management position in Miami. Soon after, she met Alex, her soon-to-be husband, and the rest is history.

To say that I was sad when she left is an understatement. I had forgotten what it was like to have someone I could open up to on that level—to have a best friend. And though it felt great to connect again, it only made me realize how much I missed Asher. The fallout from our broken relationship wasn't just about me losing the man I was in love with. It was also about losing the only person in the world who understood me completely.

It's an awful thing to say, but since then, Andrea has acted as a sort of human Splenda over the past couple of years. I love her and she's the closest thing I have to a best friend now, but she's only made me crave sugar more—the true sweetness that was my relationship with Asher.

"Missed you too," I tell her, emotion clogging my throat. "But we saw each other just a couple of months ago."

Andrea releases me from her tight grip and looks down at me skeptically. "That was in May—seven months ago, girl. It's been a minute!"

Oh. I guess it *was* a while ago...

Someone snorts behind me. "Our little Rosie doesn't really have any concept of time, does she? Or familial obligation. You haven't deigned us with your presence for Christmas since you were in college."

I could've, if you'd have celebrated it elsewhere, I want to tell her.

I turn to face Diana, who's never been subtle regarding her feelings about my life choices.

Just like our dad.

Her dark eyes narrow in my direction, curly hair stacked high in a bun atop her head. She sets the glass of wine in her hand down on the kitchen counter.

"Hey." I smile and walk over to hug her just the same, because she's my sister. Though I would happily murder her sometimes, I'd also kill anyone who dared mess with her even a little bit. "I missed you, too, Dee."

She relents, wrapping her arms around me. "Yeah, whatever." But I can sense her grin.

From the corner of my eye, I catch Asher pull a spoon out from the cutlery drawer and stick it in the giant pot of beef stew stuffing, shoveling a huge scoop into his mouth. How he didn't just burn the roof of his mouth is beyond me.

Mom runs over to him and slaps him across the chest with a potholder. "Hey! No sampling!" He playfully rolls his eyes at her, but kisses the top of her head, playing her like a fiddle. "Okay, maybe just a little, then." Asher can do no wrong in her eyes.

He smiles at her and turns to my sisters. With a little wave, he greets them as if he sees them all the time. Andrea gives him a big hug, though, thanking him for coming all the way here. "Although I know you didn't just come here for me. *Duh!*"

He laughs and pulls away, patting her once on the shoulder. My stomach lurches at the contact, my skin burning with envy. Everyone is so open and honest around him, and I'm here measuring every single word that comes out of my mouth, every expression on my face.

Feeling like crawling out of my skin, I change the topic. "Dee, where are Rodrigo and the girls? And *Pa?*" I ask, looking around, expecting to hear the loud, buoyant sounds of Diana's husband chasing their two girls around the house, my father's curt responses and disapproving glances.

Diana shrugs and picks her glass up, taking an unusually long sip of wine. "Rodrigo and Dad took the kids out to the skating rink. *Alex* went with them, too." She shoots Andrea a look.

"Oh my God, Rosie. Can you believe *Papi* is making Alex sleep at the hotel? How ridiculous is that?" Andrea dramatically rolls her eyes with a loud scoff. "I mean, forget about the fact that we're getting married in a week. We've also been *living* together back in Miami for the past year."

My mother frowns, putting her hands on her hips. "Your father and I would like to live in denial, *gracias*. And if he doesn't want your boyfriend—"

"*Fiancé.*"

"—sleeping under *his* roof, then it's *his* choice. Your father is traditional, and he doesn't think it's appropriate for an unmarried man and woman to sleep in the same bed together."

My sisters and mother argue over living in denial, but I tune them out. My eyes fly to Asher's, cheeks burning a deep red as I realize he's looking at me, too. I'd stake my life that we're both thinking of how he would regularly sneak into my bedroom late at night. Of him climbing the trellis up to my window, knocking on the glass and sliding it open, and me letting him slip into bed with me several nights a week. Years of staying up past curfew, falling asleep on his chest after binging shows or movies on my laptop, of late-night talks. Years of offering each other support, when I couldn't stand to be around anyone but him, and vice versa.

And that one final sleepover...

The feeling of his weight on me, the way his fingers grazed the skin of my thigh, how we fought to keep quiet while everyone in the house slept. His soft lips against my ear as he whispered words that, to this day, make my heart ache...

I squeeze my eyes shut, the pain in my chest knocking me breathless.

No, no, no, no.

Don't go back there.

I open my eyes to find Asher's eyes on my mouth, but they quickly flit away.

"Sorry to interrupt, but I'm beat," he says over the sudden Spanglish arguing. "And I should probably go see my mom now before heading out to return the rental."

"Of course, of course," Mom says.

And with a nod, Asher leaves the kitchen, picks up his duffel at the foot of the stairs, and softly closes the front door on his way out without even acknowledging me once.

I stare after him, a little shocked. No '*See you later*'. Nothing. *Nada.* Not even a glance in my direction.

It hurts.

Acknowledgments

This book was a fun little project that came about as an idea during a my writers' group. It was initially supposed to be a bonus chapter offered to those who signed up to my newsletter, but then... Just chatting about, inspiration struck somehow—as often happens during these sessions. So my writers' group at Quill & Cup are to thank for this here project. They offered so much support and encouragement and aaaalll of the feedback. I want to give particular shout-outs to Ania, Kase (I mean, that title, girl), Jenn, Allison, Sam, Eve, Carrie, Tracey, Elze, Mandi M, Krysann, and all the lovely women who make up the rest of the group. You were so kind and offered such great advice when I had to cancel the launch of my winter book, reminding me that it's okay, and that *bleep* happens and that it's not the end of the world.

In the end, not publishing *Second Chance Snowmance* was the right choice. I needed to give my body and mind the rest it needed. So I took a month to revisit these loved characters and give them the happily every after they deserve, with the added bonus of helping people through fundraising.

About
CAROLINE FRANK

Caroline Frank is an indie author and self-proclaimed shoe addict. She currently resides in Massachusetts with her husband and two crazy cats, Señor Kitty and Salem.

She spends her days reading, crocheting, crafting, writing, and biking. Her favorite things include the first sip of an iced-cold Coke and using self-deprecating humor to get through the day.

Though she always planned to eventually take over the world, she thinks writing fun stories every day is pretty freaking awesome and plans to continue to do so for the foreseeable future.

Also by
CAROLINE FRANK

Seasons of Love Series (Open-Door Romantic Comedy):

Fall Into You (Book 1)

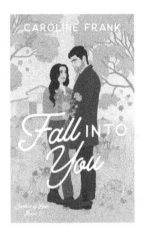

Shall We Dance? (Book 2)

Happily Ever Disaster (Novella - Book 2.5)

Second Chance Snowman (Book 3) - Coming November 23!

Second Chance
Snowmance
SEASONS OF LOVE:
BOOK 3

CAROLINE FRANK

Standalone Women's Contemporary (Open-Door):

In For a Penny

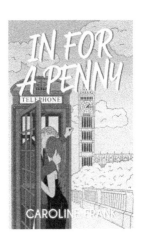

Printed in the USA
CPSIA information can be obtained
at www.ICGtesting.com
CBHW021550141024
15833CB00010B/552